Witch Is Why Promises Were Broken

Chapter 1

Sigh! Paperclips — they were the bane of my life.

It didn't matter how many times I sorted the paperclip tray, they always seemed to get mixed up again.

What? Yes, of course I realise that there are bigger problems in the world, but I was between cases, and bored out of my mind. I didn't even have Winky to distract me because he'd gone out for lunch with Peggy. How come Jack never called around to take *me* out for lunch? I would have to have words with him.

Just then, a cat jumped in through the open window. Naturally, I assumed it was Winky, but I soon realised that this particular cat had one hundred percent more eyes than my beloved feline companion. Judging by his size, this ginger obviously enjoyed his food.

"Can I help you?" I pushed the paperclip drawer closed.

"I'm looking for Winky."

"He's at lunch."

"Are you his secretary?"

"His what?" I almost choked. "Do I look like his secretary?"

"Come to think of it, probably not. From what I hear, he goes for the young, sexy type."

Cheek!

"What did you want with Winky?"

"I have a case I'd like him to investigate."

"I think you must be mistaken." I laughed. "I'm the P.I. around these parts."

"I don't think so." He produced a business card.

"Let me see that."

What the — ?

The business card was printed in a pleasing turquoise ink on textured white card—it was way better quality than the cheapo cards I used. On it was printed:

Winky P.I.
Discreet, confidential investigations.

Below that was a phone number and address. *My* phone number and address!

"Do you know what time he'll be back?" Ginger was obviously growing impatient.

"No idea, but his lunches usually drag on well into the afternoon."

He took back the business card. "I'll write my name and phone number on the back of this. Get Winky to call me, would you?"

I was still too stunned to speak, so simply took the card from him.

"Who were you talking to, Jill?"

I hadn't heard Mrs V walk into the room.

"Talking to?" I glanced across at the window, but the cat had legged it.

"I thought I heard you speaking to someone."

"Oh? I—err—I was just practising my lines."

"Lines for what?"

"Err—the—err—amateur dramatics production that Kathy has roped me into."

"How exciting. What's the production?"

"It's—err—Murder at the Vicarage."

"What part do you play?"

"Miss Marple. I'm the one who solves the mystery."

"That will make a pleasant change for you, dear."

"What do you mean? I always solve the mysteries."

"I meant for you to take part in a play."

"Oh, right. Yes, I'm looking forward to it."

"You must let me know when it's going to be on. Armi and I will definitely come to see it."

Oh bum!

"Did you want something, Mrs V?"

"Your two o' clock appointment is here."

"Oh, yes. Mr and Mrs Gander, isn't it?"

"Yes. They tell me their names are Lucy and Brucey."

"Lucy and Brucey Gander." I grinned. "You'd better show them in before they wander off."

Mrs V gave me that sympathetic look of hers.

***

Mrs Gander managed a weak smile, but Mr Gander looked as though someone had ruffled his feathers.

What? Okay, no more goose jokes. Sheesh, you lot are such spoilsports!

"Mr and Mrs Gander, please take a seat. Can I get you a drink?"

Mr Gander waved away the offer without consulting his wife; he was clearly keen to get down to business.

"My brother-in-law, Lucy's brother, Gary, died recently."

"I'm sorry to hear that."

"They say it was suicide, but that's nonsense."

"You think someone murdered him?"

"Murdered him and his wife."

"It might be best if you were to talk me through this

from the beginning."

"Gary and his wife, Gena, were on the Washbridge Flyer. Have you heard of it?"

"I can't say I have."

"It's a steam train. From what I understand, it runs most Sundays from spring through to autumn. It's mostly steam enthusiasts who travel on it, but Gary thought it would be romantic to take Gena on there. She was murdered during the journey. Her body was found in the corridor, close to the toilet; she'd been stabbed in the heart."

"And your brother-in-law?"

"They claim he jumped from the train."

"Who stabbed Gena?"

"That's just it—they reckon Gary did it, and then killed himself."

"You clearly don't believe that otherwise you wouldn't be here. What's happening with the police investigation?"

"What investigation?" He scoffed. "There is no police investigation. As far as they're concerned, Gary killed Gena, and then threw himself off the train."

"Surely, there must have been witnesses?"

"There weren't. The corridor where the toilet is located isn't visible from the main carriage. One of the other passengers found Gena's body."

"And your brother-in-law?"

"His body was found by the track."

"No one saw him jump?"

"He didn't jump!"

"Sorry."

"Whoever stabbed Gena must have fought with Gary, and pushed him off the train."

"Have you shared these thoughts with the police?"

"Of course I have, but they're not interested. That's why we've come to see you today."

"You said this happened recently? When exactly?"

"Two months ago."

"Where does the steam train run from? Washbridge station?"

"No. There's a small station at Upper Wash. It's on the main line, but the regular trains haven't called there for many years. Will you take the case, Ms Gooder?"

"It's Jill. I am rather busy at the moment, but I can see how much this means to you, so I'll make time."

The Ganders had no sooner left than Winky returned from his lunch.

"Did you manage to get all the paperclips sorted?" He was sitting on the window sill, preening himself.

"I'll have you know that while you've been taking a lazy lunch, I've just landed a new case."

"Paperclip related?"

"A double murder. Potentially."

"I guess that means you'll be able to stave off the bailiffs for another month."

"You had a visitor while you were out."

"It wasn't Jimmy The Jewels, was it? I told him I'd pay for the bracelet by the end of the month."

"What bracelet?"

"The one I bought for Peggy."

"Is it her birthday?"

"No. I don't need a reason to buy jewellery for my lady. Was it Jimmy?"

Jack really did need to take a leaf out of Winky's book.

"It wasn't Jimmy The Jewels, but it was a cat."

"Not Bella coming to beg me to take her back, I hope? She's becoming an embarrassment."

"It wasn't Bella either. He left his name and number on the back of this."

Winky jumped off the window sill, and onto my desk. When he reached for the card, I pulled it away.

"Hey, do you mind? Give it here."

"All in good time. First, I'd like you to explain this." I flipped the card over. "Since when were you a P.I?"

"Didn't I mention it? I'm sure I did."

"I'm sure you didn't. I would have remembered. What makes you think you can be a P.I?"

"Do you really need to ask? If *you* can do the job, then it stands to reason that I can."

"This is a difficult job. Not everyone is cut out for it."

"Yeah, yeah. You have to say that, but you seem to be able to wing it with little or no skills."

"And who said you could use my phone number for your business?"

"You're right. It isn't ideal. I've been meaning to talk to you about getting a second line put in. It shouldn't add much to your bill."

"Dream on, Sherlock."

***

It was Jack's turn to make dinner. Hurray!

He'd just texted to say he wouldn't be home until late. Boo!

That left me with three choices: I could make my own dinner. Or I could buy a ready-meal from the corner shop.

Or…

"Thanks for inviting me over for dinner, Kathy."

"Come in. And, as I recall, you invited yourself."

"Pah, semantics. Where's everyone?"

"Pete isn't back from work yet. Mikey's having dinner at a friend's house, and Lizzie is in her room. Actually, I'm a bit worried about her. Just lately, she's been spending more and more time in there by herself."

"Does she seem down?"

"Far from it. She's been really bubbly recently, but I still worry about her spending so much time alone in her bedroom."

"I'm sure she's fine."

"It isn't just that. She's started talking to herself."

"How do you mean?"

"A few times now, I've heard her talking when she's been alone in her room."

"Are you sure she wasn't singing? Or maybe it was the TV?"

"She doesn't have a TV in there, and she definitely wasn't singing. She seemed to be having a one-sided conversation."

"Have you spoken to her about it?"

"I've tried to, but she denied she'd been doing it. Would you have a word with her? She seems to open up to you more than she does to me."

"Sure. I'll go say hello to her now."

As soon as I walked into Lizzie's room, I could see exactly what was going on. Sitting on the bed, next to Lizzie, was Caroline—the little ghost girl from Lizzie's school.

"Hi, you two," I said, in a whisper.

"This is my Auntie Jill, Caroline."

"I know. She came to my house when I was poorly. Remember?"

"Oh yes." Lizzie giggled. "That's when you gave me Marky." She held up the ghost beanie.

"You two need to keep your voices down in here." I put my finger to my lips. "Your mummy thinks you're talking to yourself, Lizzie."

The two girls giggled.

"Mummy can't hear Caroline, can she?"

"No. Just you. That's why she thinks you're talking to yourself. Anyway, how come Caroline is here and not at the school?"

"She spends most of her time at school, but she likes to come over for sleepovers sometimes, don't you?"

Caroline nodded. "I'd never been on a sleepover until I met Lizzie."

"You won't tell Mummy, will you, Auntie Jill? She'll think I'm making it up."

"Don't worry. I won't say anything, but just remember to keep your voices down."

"Well?" Kathy said, as soon as I joined her in the kitchen. "What do you think?"

"She's absolutely fine. There's nothing to worry about."

"What about the whole talking to herself thing?"

"She isn't talking to herself. She's talking to her imaginary friend."

"Oh no! I knew it."

"Calm down. Lots of kids have imaginary friends when they're around Lizzie's age. It's perfectly natural. She'll soon grow out of it."

"I didn't have an imaginary friend."

"I did. Don't you remember Wilbur?"

"No."

"That's because you were so self-absorbed. Wilbur was my imaginary friend for a couple of years."

"Then what?"

"I grew out of him. The same will happen with Lizzie."

"Are you sure?"

"Positive, but I wouldn't mention to her that you know. It might embarrass her. She'll tell you about her friend when she's ready."

"Okay. I hope you're right."

As soon as Peter came through the door, Kathy was on him. "Well? Did you get it?"

"Let me get inside first. Hi, Jill."

"Hi."

"Come on," Kathy demanded. "Tell me."

"Yeah. I got it."

"Brilliant!" She threw her arms around him. "Does that mean I can have a new car?"

I was intrigued. "What's this all about?"

"I've just landed a contract with Washbridge Country Hall. I'll be maintaining their gardens on a regular basis. It's almost as big a contract as the Washbridge House job."

"Well done, you."

"Thanks, Jill. I just hope I don't encounter the same problems as the previous three contractors."

"I've told you," Kathy chipped in. "That's a load of old nonsense."

"What happened with the other contractors?" I asked.

"They quit because of—" He glanced at Kathy.

"You may as well tell her now that you've started."

"They quit because they said there were ghosts in the maze."

I laughed. "You don't believe in ghosts, Peter, do you?"

"No, of course not." He didn't sound very convincing.

"Guess who's going to get a new car?" Kathy beamed.

Chapter 2

The next morning, Jack was already up when I eventually managed to drag myself out of bed and downstairs.

"I thought you were going to have that steak and kidney pie for dinner last night," he said. "It's still in the fridge."

"I was going to, but then Kathy asked me to go around to her place for dinner."

"I bet she did."

"What do you mean by that?"

"It means I bet you couldn't be bothered to cook, so invited yourself over there."

"Well, that's where you're wrong. I wasn't bothered about going over there, but she insisted, and she is my sister after all."

He grinned. "So, if I give her a call, she'll confirm that, will she?"

"Of course. Go ahead if you don't believe me." I called his bluff.

"No need. I'll ask her the next time I see her."

I shrugged. "What time did you get in last night?"

"Just after midnight."

"Were you working on anything interesting?"

"Not really, but I did hear some interesting news, though."

"Oh?"

"Leo Riley has been transferred to Exeter."

"When does he leave?"

"He's already gone. His replacement starts today, apparently."

"Who is it? Anyone you know?"

"I didn't actually hear who had replaced him."

"I should go over to the police station, to introduce myself."

"I'm not sure that's a good idea."

"Why not? I'd like to get off on the right foot this time. I've got more chance of doing that if I let them know who I am and what I'm about."

"You have a bad habit of rubbing people up the wrong way."

"That's not true. When have I ever done that?"

"How long have you got? It's a long list."

"Nonsense. I think it's a good idea. I'll be charm personified."

Just then, there was a knock at the door.

"Who could that be at this time of the morning?" I grumbled. "Whoever it is, tell them to get lost."

"Charm personified, eh?" Jack started for the door. I followed him.

"Sorry to call so early." Mr Hosey smiled that crooked smile of his. "I'm trying to catch people before they go to work."

"That's no problem," Jack said.

"Tell him to sling his hook," I whispered in Jack's ear.

"Is that you, Jill?" Mr Hosey craned his neck. "I didn't see you there."

"Morning, Mr Hosey," I said, through gritted teeth. "We were just about to have breakfast."

"That's very kind of you, but I really need to get around as many houses as I can before people leave for work."

Huh?

"What can I do for you, Mr Hosey?" Jack said.

"I assume you're aware of the incident involving Bessie and that *other* train?"

"Yes. It's fortunate that no one was injured."

"It was all the fault of that idiot, Kilbride. It's just as well that he's moved out, otherwise I might have done something I'd regret. The damage to Bessie is quite extensive — she's practically a write-off."

"That's terrible," I said with as much conviction as I could muster, which wasn't much. "Still, life must go on. Well, thanks for the update — "

"I considered scrapping her, but then I thought how disappointed everyone would be."

Who was this *everyone* he spoke of?

He continued, "That's why I decided that Bessie had to be saved, and why I started the Restore Our Bessie fund." He pulled open his jacket to reveal a T-shirt, which had a picture of Bessie (in happier times) on the front. Underneath the picture were the letters: R.O.B.

Only then, did I notice the cardboard box at his feet.

"All profits from the T-shirts go to the R.O.B. fund. Now, Jack, I assume you're a large?"

"Err — that's right." Jack stuttered. "Large."

"Hold on a minute!" I stepped forward.

"Don't worry, Jill, I haven't forgotten you. Medium?"

"Small actually, but — "

"One large and one small. That will be fifty pounds."

"How much?" I gasped.

"A bargain, I know."

***

Mr Ivers was all alone in the toll booth; he didn't look

very happy.

"Where's your little helper?"

"Bert is back at college, so I'm having to do everything myself."

"By *everything*, I assume you mean collect the cash?"

"My elbows are giving me gyp already."

"Couldn't you find someone else to step into Bert's shoes?"

"I've been trying to, but it isn't easy. It's not like I can afford to pay very much. I don't suppose you'd fancy it, would you?"

"I do have my own business to run."

"You could do the odd shift between cases."

"I don't think so."

"Apart from the pay, I'd also throw in a free subscription to Toppers News."

"Tempting, but I still have to decline." I handed him the toll fee. "Have a nice day."

***

The outer office was looking so much better since Nails had redecorated. Both Mrs V and Jules were at their desks.

"Morning, Mrs V. Morning, Jules."

"Morning, Jill. Have you heard?" It was obvious that Mrs V was bursting to tell me something.

"Heard what?"

"I thought your grandmother would have told you. About the ballroom dancing competition being held in the new Ever ballroom."

"This is the first I've heard of it."

"It's going to be broadcast live on Broom TV."

"Broom? As in *sweep the floor* broom?"

"Of course not." Mrs V laughed. "Why would there be a TV station dedicated to brooms? It's actually B Room, as in Ballroom, but everyone calls it Broom. I'm surprised that you haven't heard of it with Jack being so keen on dancing."

"He spends most of his time watching TenPin TV."

"Armi and I will be entering, of course. What about you?"

"What about me?"

"Jack will want to enter, won't he?"

"I wouldn't think so. He's very busy at the moment." Plus, there was no way I was going to tell him about it.

What? I was only thinking of Jack. I just didn't want him to overdo it.

"What about you, Jules?" I said. "Will you and Gilbert be entering the competition?"

"Me?" She laughed. "I've got two left feet. And besides, the only thing that Gilbert is interested in these days is stupid bottle tops."

"How's Lules doing? Is she making any progress with the modelling?"

"She's signed with one of the agencies that Megan recommended, but so far she hasn't had any assignments. I think she's getting a little dispirited."

"She's a very pretty young woman. I'm sure the work will start to come through for her. She just needs to have a little patience."

"That's what I told her."

Winky had his head buried in a book.

"Morning, Winky. What's that you're reading?

Sleuthing for Idiots?"

He gave me a one-eyed death stare, but then went back to reading. My curiosity got the better of me, so I went over to take a closer look.

"Poker for Winners? You don't want to get into that—it's a mugs' game."

"Only if you don't know what you're doing. I've been grinding online for three months now—on the play-money tables. I'm unstoppable."

"I suppose as long as you're only playing for pretend money, it's okay."

"I've done with play-money now. I'm ready for the real thing."

"Playing online for real money is a terrible idea."

"I won't be playing online. I'll be playing live at Big Gordy's."

"Who's Big Gordy?"

"He runs the biggest game in Washbridge."

"I assume he's a cat?"

"Of course he's a cat! How am I going to get a game with humans? Be sensible."

"I still think it's a bad idea."

"You worry too much. I'm going to take that crowd to the cleaners. This time tomorrow, I'll be rolling in dough."

***

Thirty minutes later, Jules burst into my office.

"Jill! Out there! It's him!"

"Take a breath, Jules. It's who?"

"That popstar guy! Murray Murray."

"I'm not expecting him, am I?"

"No. Will you get his autograph for me?"

"I'm surprised you're a fan. Isn't he a bit old for you?"

"My mum got me into him. I love all of his stuff. Will you ask him about the autograph?"

"Sure."

"And one for my mum. She'll kill me if I don't get one for her too."

"I'll see what I can do."

"Thanks, Jill." She stood there with a silly grin on her face.

"It might be a good idea for you to show him in."

"Oh yes, of course. Right." She popped her head out of the door. "Mr Murray, would you come through, please?"

"You can call me Murray, young lady." He looked debonair as always in his white suit.

"Come and take a seat, Murray." I beckoned him in.

"Nice to see you again, Jill. Keeping busy?"

"Quite busy, yes. Can I get you anything to drink?"

"No, thanks."

Jules was still standing in the doorway, gawping at Murray.

"Thanks, Jules. That will be all."

"Okay," she said, and then mouthed, "Autographs."

Murray took a seat. "I was hoping that you might have time to do a little job for me, Jill."

"I will if I can."

"In my position, I get offered lots of strange business opportunities—most of which I turn down. But recently, my agent, Doug Cramer, came up with the idea of publishing a book."

"Your autobiography?"

"No. I've refused to do that a couple of times already.

I'm way too young to write an autobiography."

"Plenty of people do at your age, and younger."

"Maybe, and good luck to them, but I'd rather wait until I'm ready to hang up my mic before I do that. I'm actually writing a novel."

"That must be quite a challenge."

"Not really. When I say that I'm writing it, what I actually mean is that it's being written for me by a ghostwriter."

"What's the book about?"

"A popstar. What else?" He grinned. "Who just happens to be an international spy, too. It's pretty cheesy."

"So where do I come in?"

"I only agreed to go along with it on the strict understanding that no one ever found out that I'd used a ghostwriter. It would be so embarrassing if it ever got out. I went to great lengths in the contract negotiation to make sure that everyone concerned understood that."

"Sounds like you've thought it through."

"The guy who is writing it is Lorenzo Woolshape."

"I can't say I've ever heard of him."

"You won't have. He never publishes his own work; he only ever works as a ghostwriter. He's written books for loads of celebrities; he's very good. Anyway, the arrangement is that he has to write the book at my house in a room where no electronic gadgets are allowed: no phones, tablets or computers."

"What does he write on?"

"A manual typewriter. The manuscript never leaves my house. Every day, after he's finished, I lock it in the safe."

"Isn't that rather extreme?"

"Maybe, but it means there's no way the manuscript can be leaked to the press."

"So, what brings you here today?"

"I'd like you to pay a visit to the house when Lorenzo is working on the book."

"Why?"

"It's hard to explain, but if you could drop by, everything will become clear."

"Okay. When will he be there next?"

"Tomorrow afternoon. Can you make it around two o'clock?"

"Sure."

"Thanks, Jill." He stood up. "I'll see you then."

"Before you go. I wanted to ask you about an autograph."

"Of course." He took a small photo from the inside pocket of his jacket, and before I could stop him, he'd signed it: To Jill. Lots of love, Murray Murray.

"Actually, it's for my PA. The young woman who saw you in just now."

"Oh? Right, okay."

"Her name is Jules. Oh, and she'd like one for her mother too. Perhaps you could check what her mother's name is on your way out."

"No problem." He glanced at the photo that he'd already signed. "What shall I do with this one?"

"I—err—I'll keep that, obviously. Thanks."

Murray had no sooner left than Winky jumped onto my desk.

"What are you going to do with that?" He pointed to the signed photo.

"Throw it in the bin, probably."

"I'll have it."

"I didn't realise you were a Murray Murray fan."

"I'm not. I can't stand that awful row, but Peggy loves him. This will put me in her good books for sure."

"But it says: To Jill."

He grabbed a pair of scissors, and chopped off the top of the photo — above Murray Murray's head.

"Now it doesn't."

Chapter 3

I had an appointment with Luther at my office; we'd arranged to go over my quarterly accounts. When he arrived, he looked very pleased with himself.

"Are my accounts that good?" I asked, enthusiastically.

"Your accounts? No, sorry, they're terrible as usual."

"But when you came in just now, you were beaming."

"I've just heard that I've been nominated as one of the finalists in the regional accountant of the year award." He passed me a sheet of paper which had a list of the four finalists.

"Seymour Sums?" I laughed. "That has to be a made-up name."

"It isn't. Seymour is probably the favourite to win."

"Are these awards a big deal?"

"Extremely. They're very prestigious. If I was to win, it would mean a lot more business would come my way."

"I'm sure you'll win. How's Maria?"

"She's okay, but I'm not sure she'll stick with the job at Ever for much longer."

"My grandmother did rather pull the rug out from under her feet by changing the shop so dramatically."

"I don't think it would have been quite so bad if it wasn't for that awful red trouser suit she has to wear."

"The Everette uniform? It isn't a good look, is it?" I tried not to laugh, but I couldn't stop myself.

"It really isn't." Luther dissolved into laughter too.

***

Despite Jack's misgivings, I still thought it would be a

good idea to introduce myself to Leo Riley's replacement. My history with the police force to-date had not been great—understatement of the year! Maybe, if this time I took the initiative and made it clear that I wanted to work alongside them, and to co-operate whenever I could, then surely that would pay dividends.

"Yes? What can I do for you?" The sergeant behind the desk at Washbridge police station looked as though he wanted to be anywhere but there.

"Hi!" I treated him to my sweetest smile. "I'd like a word with Leo Riley's replacement, please."

"Do you have an appointment?"

"No, but I was hoping that he could spare me just a couple of minutes. That's all I need."

"Who are you? And what's it in connection with?"

This guy was such a charmer.

"My name is Jill Gooder; I'm a—"

"Gooder? I know who you are. Take a seat over there."

That didn't sound good. He disappeared into the back, and when he returned a few minutes later, he pointed at me. "She's over there."

From behind the sergeant, there appeared a familiar face.

"Sushi?"

Susan Shay had worked alongside Jack for a brief period. She and I had not exactly hit it off.

"It's Detective Shay, to you. What are you doing here, Gooder?"

"I—err—"

"I hear that you and Jack Maxwell are together now?"

"That's right."

"Well, while you're here, I want to make one thing

crystal clear. I'm not a soft touch like Jack. If I find out that you have interfered in any of my cases, I'll throw your sorry backside in jail. Got it?"

"Loud and clear." I started for the door. "Nice to see you again, Sushi."

That went exceedingly well.

***

The excursions on the Washbridge Flyer were run by a company called Washbridge Steam Ltd. The director of the company was a Mr Desmond Sidings who had agreed to spare me a few minutes to discuss the tragic deaths of Gena and Gary Shore. Mr Sidings' office was located on Upper Wash railway station.

I tried his office door, but it was locked. I knocked a couple of times, but there was no response. The station was now used only for the weekly steam train excursions, so I wasn't too surprised that it appeared to be deserted. I was just about to leave when I spotted someone at the far end of the opposite platform. A man, dressed in blue overalls, was watering the flower baskets. To get to that side of the track I had to use a rather rusty footbridge, which was in dire need of a lick of paint.

"Excuse me," I called to the man. "Could you tell me where I'll find Mr Desmond Sidings?"

"Are you Jill Gooder?"

"That's right. Mr Sidings?"

"That's me. Call me Desmond. Shall we go to my office?"

"I don't mind talking to you while you work."

"No need. I'm done here. Come on. We'll be warmer

inside."

Once we were in his office, he discarded the blue overalls to reveal a rather pleasing tweed suit.

"Now, Jill, you mentioned on the phone that you wanted to discuss the tragic deaths that occurred on The Flyer?"

"That's right."

"You do realise that the police have already concluded that the man murdered his wife and then committed suicide?"

"Yes. I understand that's what the police believe happened."

"Is there any reason for you to think otherwise?"

"At this stage, I have an open mind. I'm working for Brucey and Lucy Gander. The deceased male was Lucy Gander's brother."

"I see. And how exactly can I help you?"

"My clients don't believe that Gary Shore was capable of murder, and they totally reject the notion that he would have killed his wife. I've been asked to look into this tragic incident, to see if I can find evidence of foul play."

"Don't you think if there had been foul play, the police would have found some evidence?"

"In an ideal world, yes, but in my experience, that isn't always the case. I'd like to speak to all of the passengers who were on the train that day if you could let me have their details?"

"I'm very sorry, but that's impossible because we don't record the passenger's details when we sell day tickets; there's no reason for us to do it. We do have a small number of season ticket holders—steam enthusiasts who take the trip regularly."

"Were there any season ticket holders on that particular trip?"

"Just two: Stanley Sidcup and Barbara Hawthorne."

"Could you let me have their details?"

"I can give you their phone numbers. It would be up to them whether they'd be willing to talk to you."

"That would be great, thanks. Were you on the train that day, Desmond?"

"No. I don't miss many, but that particular day, I had a mountain of paperwork to catch up on."

***

What I needed was a nice cup of tea and some yummy cake, so I magicked myself over to Aunt Lucy's house where I could hear voices coming from the lounge. When I popped my head around the door, I was appalled to see Alicia sitting on the sofa with Aunt Lucy; they were both enjoying a cup of tea.

"Jill." Aunt Lucy greeted me with her customary smile. "Come in. Help yourself to a cup of tea."

"Hi, Jill." Alicia smiled.

"Hi." I couldn't bring myself to reciprocate.

What on earth was Alicia doing there? I quickly poured myself a cup of tea, and joined them.

"Help yourself to one of these." Aunt Lucy offered me the plate of delicious-looking cupcakes. "Alicia made them."

"Not for me, thanks. I'm not hungry."

"More for us then." Aunt Lucy picked one up, and was about to take a bite when I knocked it out of her hand.

"Jill?" She looked genuinely shocked. "What do you

think you're doing?"

"You can't trust her." I pointed an accusing finger at Alicia. "Have you forgotten that she tried to poison me?"

"It's okay, Lucy." Alicia stood up; she looked close to tears. "Jill's right. I don't deserve your trust. I'd better be going."

When Aunt Lucy and I were alone, she said, "I understand that you and Alicia have history, Jill, but I really think you need to let it go."

"She tried to kill me!"

"I know, but Alicia has explained that she was under Ma Chivers' control. I don't think she had any option but to carry out her orders."

"I don't buy that. Not for one minute. For all you know, these cupcakes could be poisoned."

"They aren't. I know because Alicia brought them around yesterday. I've already eaten two of them, and I'm perfectly okay."

Aunt Lucy might be prepared to trust her, but it would take a long time for me to do it—if I ever did.

Fortunately, Aunt Lucy had a new packet of custard creams, so I made do with four of those instead of cake.

What? Of course four isn't excessive. Sheesh!

"By the way, Jill, I have some news to tell you. Lester has completed his training and is now fully qualified."

"He must be pleased."

"He's delighted.

"What about you? How do you feel about the whole grim reaper thing now?"

"I'm slowly coming around to the idea, but I still try not to think about it in too much detail."

"Will you be celebrating?"

"Actually, Lester and I are going out with Monica for dinner tonight."

"With Monica?"

"Yes. I don't mind admitting that I was completely wrong about that young lady. She's a really nice person, and I'm pleased that Lester had her as his mentor. Of course, now that he's qualified, he'll be working solo. In fact, he's waiting to find out which area he's been allocated; he should hear within the next few days."

After leaving Aunt Lucy's, I magicked myself back to the office where Winky was still reading his poker book. I'd only been in there a few minutes when the temperature in the room suddenly dropped. Moments later, my mother appeared and took the chair opposite me.

"What's wrong, Mum? You don't look very happy."

"I'm not. It's that stupid husband of mine."

"What's Alberto done now?"

"He wants to open up our garden to visitors, and to charge them to see the gnomes."

"What's wrong with that?" I laughed. "I thought you liked the gnomes?"

"Not particularly. I try to be supportive of Alberto's hobby, but this is taking it way too far."

"You don't need to get involved with the visitors, do you? Couldn't you just stay in the house out of the way?"

"If only. Alberto wants me to be the tour guide."

"Why can't he do that himself? He knows more about the gnomes than anyone else."

"He doesn't think anyone will be able to understand his Welsh accent. What if your father finds out about this? I'll never hear the end of it."

"Speaking of my father, did you ever apologise for accusing him of stealing Alberto's gnomes?"

"I think so." She was deliberately avoiding eye contact.

"Mum! Did you?"

"I won't apologise to that man. Anyway, I didn't come here to complain about Alberto and his gnomes. I need your help."

"Oh?"

"For a friend of mine: Sonya Aynos. Her husband has gone missing, and she's really worried. If I give you her address in GT, would you pay her a visit?"

"Sure. Or she could come to see me here?"

"Sonya doesn't *do* the human world. She reckons it brings her out in blotches."

"Okay. I'll try and get over there later today, or tomorrow at the latest."

"Thanks, Jill."

My mother had no sooner disappeared than Mad turned up at my office, suitcase in hand.

"Are you leaving already?"

"Yeah. I wasn't expecting to be going so soon, but there was a vacancy in London, and I didn't want to miss out on it."

"How has your mum taken it?"

"She doesn't actually know yet. I realise that makes me a coward, but I just couldn't face telling her that I was actually going, so I waited until she and Nails were out, and then left her a note."

"That's really not very nice, Mad."

"I know, but it's done now. You can tell her that you did

your best to persuade me to stay, but that I was determined to move to London. You will come and visit me, won't you, Jill?"

"Of course I will."

We hugged for the longest time, and then she left.

I was going to miss Mad.

Chapter 4

Mad had no sooner left than I got a call from Amber.

"Jill, there's someone here in Cuppy C, asking to see you."

"Who is it?"

"His name is Timothy; he says he knows you. Can you pop over?"

To the best of my knowledge, I didn't know anyone by the name of Timothy.

"Are you sure he knows me?"

"He says so. Look, I have to go. Pearl isn't in today, and I'm run off my feet. Shall I tell him you can't see him?"

"No, don't do that. I'll be straight over."

Amber was holding the fort behind the tea room counter all by herself. When she spotted me out of the corner of her eye, she gestured to a table at the back of the room. Seated there was Timothy the troll! It had never occurred to me for one moment that it might be him.

"You wanted to see me?"

"That was quick. Thanks for coming over. Can I get you a drink?"

His demeanour was very different to the last time I'd encountered him. Back then, he'd been quite aggressive, and had held Magna Mondale's book for ransom until I supplied him with some starlight fairy wings.

"No, thanks. There's a queue a mile long. What can I do for you?" I pulled up a chair and joined him at the table.

"It's my cousin, Cole."

"Cole the troll?" I laughed.

Timothy shot me a look.

"Sorry. You were saying?"

"Cole is having a spot of bother. I told him about you, and he asked if I'd get in touch with you."

"Why didn't he contact me himself?"

"Cole is very timid; he's much too scared to come into town."

"Does Cole live down a well, too?"

"You already know perfectly well that I don't *live* down a well. That's just my place of work."

"Sorry. Does Cole work down a well, too?"

"No. He's a bridge troll. Cushy number, if you ask me. He gets to bask in the sunlight and fresh air while I'm stuck down a dark hole. Anyway, I digress. Cole would like you to pay him a visit."

"What's it in connection with?"

"It would be best if he explained it himself."

"Okay. Does he live near to you in Troll Crescent?"

"No, why would he? Do you live in the same street as all of your relatives?"

"No, I just thought — sorry."

"He'd like you to visit him at his place of work if that's possible. I'll give you the address."

"Okay. I'll pop over to see him as soon as I get the chance."

Timothy gave me the address of his cousin's bridge, and then he left. I was about to leave too when I noticed that the queue at the counter had finally subsided. Amber looked shell-shocked.

"It looks like you've been run off your feet," I said.

"No kidding. Pearl has really dropped me in it."

"Where is she?"

"I wish I knew. She rang first thing this morning, to say

she had something urgent to attend to, and that she'd be in later."

"Is she okay?"

"She sounded just fine. If she's skived off to go shopping, I won't be best pleased."

"I suppose I ought to be making tracks."

"Hold on, Jill. There's something I want to tell you."

"Go on."

"I really shouldn't."

"Okay."

"But I have to tell someone or I'm going to burst."

"Spit it out, then."

She glanced over at the cake counter where two of her assistants were chatting to one another. "Nadine! Can you watch the tea room for a few minutes?"

Amber led me into the back of the shop.

"If I tell you, you have to promise not to breathe a word to anyone."

"Okay."

"Not to Mum, and definitely not to Pearl."

"Okay."

"Say you promise, and cross your heart."

"Sheesh! I promise. Cross my heart."

"I don't know if I should. I promised William that I wouldn't."

"Okay, then."

"I'm pregnant!"

"What?"

"I'm pregnant. I found out yesterday."

"Are you sure?"

"Positive. I went to see the doctor last night after work. I told Pearl I was meeting William to go shopping."

"Why don't you want Pearl to know?"

"She and Alan have been trying for a baby too. I'm worried about how she'll react when she finds out."

"She'll be happy for you, I'm sure."

"You're probably right. I am going to tell her and Mum, just not yet, so you can't say anything. William will kill me."

"My lips are sealed. Congratulations. It's wonderful news. I couldn't be happier for you."

* * *

It was always the same with my business: feast or famine. Yesterday, I'd had no work; now, I'd landed the Gander case, I'd been asked by my mother to help her friend, I'd promised to help Murray Murray, and I'd had a request to assist a troll. Quite the caseload.

I decided to visit my mother's friend first, so I magicked myself over to GT where Sonya Aynos lived in a mid-terrace house close to Poltergeist Park. I had nothing against dreamcatchers, but I couldn't help but feel that Sonya had overdone it a tad. It took me several minutes to fight my way through them all.

I'd no sooner knocked than she opened the door.

"Sonya? I'm Jill Gooder."

"Hi. Darlene called to say she'd spoken to you, but I wasn't expecting you to come around so soon."

"It sounded important."

"It is. Come on in."

"You have a lot of dreamcatchers."

"It's the only way to make sure I don't have nightmares. I tried just one, and that didn't work. Nor did two or three. In the end, I found I needed twenty-seven. They seem to do the job."

"Right."

Ten minutes later, we were settled in the living room, with a nice cup of tea and Sonya's home-made shortbread biscuits, which were perfectly nice, but no substitute for custard creams.

"My mother said that your husband has gone missing?"

"That's right. I'm very worried, Jill."

"Do you suspect foul play?"

"No, I don't think so. I'm afraid it may be my fault."

"How do you mean?"

"Malcolm worked at the garden gnome factory, but a couple of weeks back, he was let go along with another ten men."

"Let go? Why?"

"The demand for garden gnomes is at an all-time low. They've had to cut back on production."

"You said you thought it might be your fault?"

"Yes. I gave him a hard time because I didn't think he was doing enough to find another job. It was totally unfair of me because he was doing the best he could. I was just stressed out by the money situation. I was worried about losing the house."

"What happened exactly?"

"One morning, I found him in here, lazing around—just watching TV, and I kind of exploded. I told him to get out and not to come back until he'd found another job. I haven't seen or heard from him since then."

"How long ago was that?"

"Just over a week. If he's done something stupid, I'll never forgive myself."

"We all say things we don't mean in the heat of an argument. I'm sure he'll be okay. Does he have any friends?"

"Not many. Malcolm isn't really one for socialising. There are two men he knocks around with occasionally: Phillip Long and Roy Wright."

"Do you have their phone numbers?"

"Yes, I'll get them for you. Do you think you'll be able to find Malcolm?"

"I'll do my very best."

***

On the drive home, I was still thinking about Amber. Ditzy as she was, I was convinced she'd make a great mum. Although I was sure that Pearl would be happy for her sister, it was bound to cause a few problems for her at Cuppy C. Would Amber go back to work after the baby was born, or would she choose to be a stay-at-home mum? Either way, Pearl was going to need more help in the shop — even if it was only for a short period of time.

Jack was already home when I got back; he looked like the cat that got the cream.

"Best news ever!" He greeted me, as soon as I walked through the door.

"Custard creams are on two for one?"

"Much better than that. I'm surprised you haven't already heard. Ever is holding a ballroom dancing competition!"

"I'm still waiting to hear the *best-ever news* that you promised me."

"That's it. Opening that ballroom was a stroke of genius by your grandmother."

"Look, Jack, I know you'll want us to enter the competition, but I really don't fancy it."

"That's okay."

"It is? I thought you'd be disappointed."

"We couldn't enter even if you wanted to."

"Why not?"

"Guess who's been asked to be one of the judges?"

"You? Really? When?"

"Your grandmother called me earlier today. She said I'd be perfect for it."

"Good for you."

"I thought we should celebrate."

"Sounds good."

"With some fish and chips."

"You really know how to push the boat out, don't you?"

"If we stay in, it's your turn to cook dinner."

"Fish and chips sounds like a great idea."

The last time we'd been to the fish and chip shop was on the day it first opened. On that occasion, the queue had been out of the door. It was much quieter this time; there were only three or four people ahead of us.

"It looks like Tish and Chip must have taken on some staff," Jack said. "These two are a right pair of weirdos. I reckon that woman has some kind of catsuit on under her smock." He laughed.

Only one person I knew would wear that ensemble. I glanced past Jack, and sure enough, there was Daze. Behind her, watching the chip fryer, was none other than Blaze. There was no sign of either Tish or Chip.

"Jack." I nudged him. "It looks like they're out of chips. Why don't you go home, butter some bread and set the table while I wait here?"

"Okay. I'll open a bottle of wine too. After all, we are celebrating."

"Great idea."

A few minutes later, I reached the front of the queue.

"Jill?" Daze looked surprised to see me. "I'd forgotten you lived in this neck of the woods." She turned to Blaze. "Can you serve for a couple of minutes?"

"Sure. Oh, hey, Jill."

"Hiya."

Daze and I moved to the far end of the counter.

"This has to be our worst assignment ever," she said.

"Are you kidding? Working in a fish and chip shop would be my idea of heaven."

"You're welcome to it. I can't get the smell of fish out of my catsuit. And just the sight of mushy peas makes me want to throw up."

"Wash your mouth out. Don't you know that mushy peas are the nectar of the gods? What are you doing here, anyway?"

"Gargoyles."

"Sorry?"

"We're having a spot of gargoyle trouble."

"How do you mean?"

"There are a few rogue gargoyles we need to round up."

"Hang on. Aren't gargoyles those stone things on old buildings?"

"Gargoyles are actually sups. They're able to live in the human world undetected by hiding in plain sight on the side of buildings."

"So, you're telling me that gargoyles are alive?"

"Of course they are; they're living, breathing sups. They're just very good at standing still."

"I never would have guessed. What have they been doing to bring themselves to your attention?"

"The majority of gargoyles are law abiding. Criminally ugly, but law abiding. This crowd, though, have been helping themselves to valuables from a number of stately homes in this area."

"I still don't get why you're working in here."

"Gargoyles have a penchant for fish and chips."

"It so obvious when you say it."

"What can I get for you, Jill?" Blaze called. He'd just finished serving his last customer.

"Can I get fish and chips twice, and a carton of mushy peas, please?"

"Open or wrapped?"

"Wrapped, please."

"Salt and vinegar?"

"Yes, please. Plenty of vinegar."

I handed over the cash, and was about to leave when Daze called me back.

"Can I interest you in any curtains?"

"What is it with the soft furnishings?"

"Beats me, but the owners insist that we try to push them."

Chapter 5

It couldn't possibly be morning already. I reached for my phone, which was on the bedside cabinet, only to find that it was five-past-six. Why was I awake at this hour? Something must have woken me. And where was Jack? He hadn't mentioned that he would be going in early.

As I stumbled down the stairs, I could hear the sound of the TV coming from the lounge. What was that doing on at this unearthly hour?

"Jack? What's going on?"

"Shush! Just a minute. I need to watch this part closely."

It took a few moments for my eyes to focus, but then I realised he was watching ballroom dancing.

"What on earth is this?"

"Just one more minute. Oh, that is quite superb." He muted the TV, and turned to me. "Sorry? What did you say?"

"I asked what you were watching."

"It's Broom TV. I don't know why I haven't watched it before. It's amazing. Did you see that last couple? Such fantastic footwork."

"Yeah. Great. But why are you watching it at stupid o'clock? It woke me up."

"I'm sorry. I hadn't realised it was so loud, but I do need to hone my observation skills ahead of the big competition."

"It's only Grandma's silly little competition."

"How can you say that when it's going to be broadcast live on Broom TV? Don't you realise what that means?"

"That a couple of people and their dog might see it?"

"Broom TV has an audience which numbers into the

tens of thousands, and they'll all be watching me. If I mess up, my reputation will be in ruins."

"Does that mean that you plan to do this every morning until a week on Sunday?"

"Yes, but I promise to keep the volume down from now on."

"Seeing as how you disturbed my beauty sleep, the least you can do is make breakfast."

"Fair enough. Toast?"

"You're not getting off that lightly. I'll have a full English."

Say what you like about Jack, but he did make the best full English in Smallwash. He had to shoot off straight after breakfast; I followed twenty minutes later.

"Hi, Clare. Hi, Tony," I said to the man-sized banana and pear that were in next door's garden.

"Morning, Jill," the banana, AKA Tony, greeted me.

"Hiya." The pear waved.

"Another con this weekend, I assume?"

"Yes. Can you guess what it is?"

"I'd say FruitCon, but I guess that's too obvious."

"Way too obvious. It's actually SlotCon."

"What's that?"

"It celebrates all manner of slot machines. We're getting together with a few friends—collectively we'll be the fruit machine symbols."

"Of course. It's so obvious now."

"Actually, Jill. A couple of people have dropped out, which means we've lost our cherries. I don't suppose you and Jack would take their places, would you? We could provide you with the costumes."

"Thanks for the offer, but we've arranged to visit Jack's parents. Good luck with it, though."

I was just about to reverse off the drive when I got a call from Grandma. She asked — or to be more accurate — told me to call in at Ever on my way into work. The morning was just getting better and better: I'd been woken at the crack of dawn by the sound of ballroom dancing, then accosted by a couple of giant fruits, and now I'd have to face Grandma. I had my fingers crossed that she wouldn't be treating her bunions when I got there. There's only so much one person can bear.

When I stopped at the toll booth, Mr Ivers had one arm in a sling.

"Oh dear. How did you break your arm?"

"It isn't broken." He took it out of the sling just to prove the point. "I'm using this to rest my elbow. I put one arm in the sling for an hour, and then I swap to the other arm."

"Does it help?"

"A little, but I'd still prefer to find someone to take the cash for me. I don't suppose you've reconsidered my offer, have you?"

"Sorry, it's not for me."

***

The door to Ever was locked when I got there; the Everettes obviously weren't early starters. When Grandma let me in, I was relieved to see she was wearing shoes — the potential bunion crisis had been averted.

She led me through to her office.

"I suppose Jack has told you I've asked him to be a

judge at the competition."

"He has. He's very excited."

"And honoured to, I would hope?"

"That goes without saying."

"This is the inaugural competition, so we're expecting a big crowd and a massive TV audience. Jack will have to hire a top of the range dress suit."

"He already has a nice charcoal suit that—"

"No, that won't do at all. Tell him to call me, and I'll give him the name of a suitable dress hire establishment."

"I assume you'll be covering his expenses?"

"In your dreams." She cackled. "And you'll need to spruce yourself up too. We can't have you letting the side down."

"I'll do my best. Now, what was it you wanted to see me about?"

"I want an update on the witchfinder situation. Have you spoken to Yvonne yet?"

"No. It isn't really something we can discuss on the phone."

"This is urgent, Jill. They could already be living among us here in Washbridge."

"Don't panic. Jack and I are going to Yvonne's on Saturday."

"Good. In the meantime, keep your eyes peeled for any new or unusual characters. You have to be on your guard. I assume you still have the Brewflower?"

"Yes, I've still got several syringes left from the last encounter with a witchfinder."

"Do you have it with you now?"

"Well, no, not at the moment. It's in the drawer at work."

"A lot of good that will do if the witchfinder attacks you. You must keep it with you at all times."

"Okay. I will."

When I came out of Grandma's office, Kathy was in the tea room; she was a vision in red.

"I never get tired of seeing you in that outfit." I chuckled.

"Shut it! I'm not in the mood this morning."

"What's wrong?"

"The kids have been driving me insane. Lizzie was talking to herself in her bedroom again. I'm beginning to think that I should take her to see the doctor."

"Don't be silly. I told you what that's all about. She just has an imaginary friend. It's really nothing to worry about."

"Maybe. And Mikey decided it would be a good idea to practise his fly-fishing cast in the living room. He managed to hook that favourite vase of mine."

"You mean the ugly one, on the mantelpiece?"

"It wasn't ugly."

"Wasn't?"

"It's in a thousand pieces now."

"You must have been glad to get out of the house and come to work, then?"

"Oh yeah. I love being run off my feet while dressed like this. What brings you down here at this time of the morning, anyway?"

"I was summoned by Grandma. I assume you've heard that she's roped Jack into being one of the judges for the ballroom dancing competition."

"I have. How does he feel about that?"

"He's over the moon. He was up at the crack of dawn so that he could watch Broom TV. Oh well, I suppose I should get going before the rest of the Everettes arrive." I hesitated. "I've just had a thought: With a name like the Everettes, you guys should start your own dance troupe. You could give The Coven a run for their money."

If looks could kill.

Snigger.

***

Jules, Lules and Gilbert were in the outer office, but none of them seemed to notice my arrival because they were too busy arguing. At first glance, it appeared that Lules and Gilbert were siding against Jules.

"Hey! Timeout!" I shouted.

"Sorry, Jill." Jules was red in the face.

"What's going on?"

"I'm trying to talk some sense into my sister, and *he* isn't helping." She pointed an accusing finger at Gilbert.

"I don't need your help or your advice!" Lules barked. "I'm not a child."

"Then stop acting like one."

"Enough!" I raised my hand. "Will someone please tell me what this is all about? Jules?"

"Lules has entered the Miss Bottle Top competition. I've told her that it's demeaning, and that she shouldn't be making a show of herself."

"It isn't demeaning at all," Lules insisted. "And besides, it will be good for my career. The people at the modelling agency have told me that I need to raise my profile if I want to get work."

"Not like this!" Jules shouted.

"There's nothing demeaning about this type of competition. They're not like they used to be years ago. These days, it's as much about personality and product knowledge as it is about looks."

"Jules is right," Gilbert chipped in.

"*You* can be quiet!" Jules slapped him down. "This is all your fault. If you hadn't given Lules the idea, she wouldn't be in this mess."

"I'm not in a mess. I'm in a competition, and nothing you or anyone else says, is going to change my mind."

"I wash my hands of you, then." Jules stood up and stormed out.

"She'll get over it," Gilbert said.

I wasn't so sure.

"I actually came to see you, Jill," Lules said.

"Oh?"

"When I won the Miss Black Pudding competition, I already had all the product knowledge I needed to get me through that part of the contest. Bottle tops are different. I know next to nothing about them."

"Can't Gilbert help you with that?"

"Yes, but only so far. What I really need is an expert. That's why I thought of you."

"Me? I don't know anything about bottle tops."

"No, but you know the guy who owns Top Of The World, don't you?"

"Norman? Yeah, I know him."

"I was hoping that you might have a word with him. Ask if he'd be willing to tutor me ahead of the competition."

"If your mind is made up, then yes, I'll have a word

with him for you."

"Thanks, Jill. You're a star."

**

When I went through to my office, I expected Winky to be waiting for me, demanding to be fed, but there was no sign of him.

"Winky?"

No response.

I crouched down, and looked under the sofa. A single eye was looking back at me.

"Are you alone?" he whispered.

"Of course I am."

"Are you sure?"

"Positive."

He crept forward, gingerly—all the time, glancing back and forth around the room.

"What's going on, Winky?"

"Nothing." He shrugged.

"Don't give me that. You look scared."

"Don't be silly. I'm perfectly—"

Winky shot back under the sofa because he'd heard something clatter in the outer office—it was probably Jules throwing something at Gilbert.

"Don't let them get me." He sounded terrified.

"Don't let *who* get you?"

"Anyone. If they ask, you haven't seen me. Tell them I've left the country."

I walked over to the office door, and peeked out. Just as I'd suspected, Jules and Gilbert were fighting again.

"It's only Jules and her boyfriend." I went back to

crouching next to the sofa.

"Are you sure?"

"Positive. Now, why don't you come on out, and tell me what this is all about?"

"You were right," he said.

Now I knew something was seriously amiss. Winky never admitted I was right about anything.

"About what?"

"I should never have got involved with that evil game."

"Poker?"

"Yeah."

"I did warn you. What happened?"

"It was all going great. I'd trebled my money."

"But?"

"But then, I got a full house: tens over sixes. So naturally, I went all in."

"And?"

"Big Gordy had a straight flush."

"Oh dear."

"He cheated. I'm sure of it. It was a set-up."

"Can you prove that?"

"Of course not."

"So, you lost all of your money. That's a lesson learned."

"It's much worse than that. Big Gordy lent me some cash."

"You borrowed money to continue to play? That was a terrible idea."

"I thought I could win."

"But you didn't?"

"No. I lost big time, and now I'm in the hole to Big Gordy for over a grand."

"You lost a grand of his money? Are you insane?"

"No, but I'll be dead when Big Gordy gets a hold of me. I was meant to pay him first thing this morning, but I don't have that kind of cash to hand."

"With all the money-making schemes that you run? You must have."

"The money is all tied up. I can't get my hands on the cash that quickly. I'll just have to lay low until I've raised the money plus interest. In the meantime, if a big, fat, ugly cat comes around here—"

"I haven't seen you?"

"Got it in one."

Chapter 6

I'd managed to contact the two season ticket holders who had been on the Washbridge Flyer when Gena and Gary Shore died. Both of them had agreed to talk to me.

Stanley Sidcup was a retired banker. He lived in Top Wash; one of the most expensive suburbs of Washbridge. His house, although obviously worth a ton of money, was seriously ugly. The house's nameplate was shaped like a train, and when I pressed the doorbell, it didn't ring a bell, but made the sound of a steam engine.

"You must be Miss Gooder." Sidcup answered the door, wearing a smoking jacket, which had a steam train motif.

"Call me Jill, please."

"Spiffing. And you must call me Stanley." He stepped to one side. "Do come in. Can I get you anything to drink? Scotch? Wine?"

"It's a little early for me."

"Quite. A cup of tea, then?"

"That would be lovely."

"Spiffing. Momsy! Are you there?"

A grey-haired woman appeared from a door at the far side of the hall. "You called, Popsy?"

"Momsy. This young lady is Jill Gooder. She's here to talk to me about the Washbridge Flyer incident."

"Terrible business." The woman frowned. "Yours must be a difficult job, dear?"

"It can be."

Although no formal introductions had been made, I was working on the assumption that Momsy and Popsy were man and wife.

"Momsy," Stanley said. "Would you make some tea for us? How do you take yours, Jill?"

"Milk and two-thirds spoonfuls of sugar, please."

"And biscuits?"

"Do you have any custard creams?"

"Sorry. Everything but. They bring Popsy out in a rash, don't they, dear?"

"Always have done."

Freak!

"Just the tea then, thanks."

Stanley led the way through to a large reception room, which was filled with all manner of railway memorabilia.

"My one vice," he said, as he ushered me into a leather armchair. "I've spent a small fortune on this stuff, but a man has to have a hobby, doesn't he?"

I nodded, and an image of Jack's bowling shirts popped into my head. What was it with men and their stupid hobbies?

"So, Jill? How can I help?"

Before I could answer, Momsy brought the tea through. "Would you like me to stay?" she asked, once she'd passed the drinks to us.

"Were you on The Flyer that day, too?"

"Goodness, no. I have better things to do with my Sundays. I was playing bridge at my club."

"In that case, it's just Stanley I need to speak to."

"Jolly good. Well, it was nice to meet you, Jill. Don't let Popsy bore you to death, telling you about his collection."

"Nice to meet you, too."

Stanley took out a pipe, and popped it into his mouth. Great! I loved being choked by tobacco smoke.

"Don't worry, Jill. I never light it. I smoked a pipe for

thirty years until Momsy put her foot down and made me stop. She said she didn't want me popping my clogs before she did. I haven't lit it for over three years, but I still find it helps me to relax, just having it in my mouth. You don't mind, do you?"

"Of course not."

"So, how can I help, exactly?"

"I understand from Desmond Sidings that you have a season ticket for The Flyer. That must be quite expensive?"

"I suppose it is, but what else am I going to spend my money on at my age? Momsy has her bridge and her ladies' lunches; I have my steam train."

"Can you tell me about that day? Did you see the couple who died?"

"Yes, I was in the same carriage as them. They were celebrating their wedding anniversary, or so he said. When they came onto the train, they were weighed down with champagne, flowers and chocolates."

"Did they both seem okay?"

"The man was very loud, but the woman seemed subdued. I thought perhaps she was embarrassed by all the fuss he was making."

"Were you seated near to them?"

"Right across the aisle. The man asked if I'd take a photo of them on his phone, and I agreed, but then he noticed my camera." Stanley grinned. "When I said I only had the one vice, I was lying. I'm something of a photography buff too. Anyway, he said that as it was a special occasion, they should have a 'proper' photo. He asked if I'd take a picture of them with my camera, and email him a copy."

"Did you take one?"

"Yes, but I have to say, she didn't seem very keen. It took me all of my time just to get her to smile."

"What happened after that?"

"Things were okay for the first part of the journey. The man was knocking back the champagne, but the woman didn't seem to be interested. Then, just about halfway through the journey, they started arguing."

"Could you hear what it was about?"

"Not really, but it soon descended into a full-scale shouting match. She started crying, and then she stormed out of the carriage towards the lavatory. He followed her. I never saw them again. I assumed they must be carrying on the argument in the corridor, or that they'd gone through to the buffet car. The next thing I knew was when someone said that a woman's body had been found." Stanley took a long suck on his unlit pipe.

"It must have been upsetting."

"Terribly. I wasn't sure I'd ever want to ride The Flyer again, but Momsy said I was just being silly. She was the one who made me get back on the horse."

Stanley's account of that day had done nothing to rule out the possibility that Gary Shore might have murdered his wife, and then committed suicide, because there had obviously been some kind of falling out just prior to the incident.

"Thank you very much for taking the time to speak to me, Stanley. Is there any chance you could let me have a copy of the photo you took?"

"Certainly. It's been a pleasure to talk to you. I don't often get the chance to spend time with a pretty, young woman." He glanced at the door. "You won't tell Momsy I said that, will you?"

"My lips are sealed."

***

Barbara Hawthorne lived in a pretty bungalow in the Washtide Retirement Village.

"Do come in, Ms Gooder. I hope you'll excuse the mess."

There was no mess; it looked like a show house.

"Thank you for seeing me, Mrs Hawthorne."

"You must call me Thorny. Everyone does."

"Okay, and I'm Jill. I wanted to speak to you because you're one of only two season ticket holders who were on the Washbridge Flyer when the Shores died."

"That's correct. How remiss of me; I haven't offered you a drink. Would you like tea or coffee?"

I settled for coffee, but passed on the shortbread biscuits.

"Are you a steam train enthusiast, Thorny?"

"Goodness no, but my late husband was. He lived for them. He used to go on The Flyer regularly, and I'd accompany him occasionally. I find that the sounds and smell of the train remind me of him. Silly, I know."

"Not at all. Which carriage were you in?"

"The rear carriage, so I didn't even see the couple who died. I'm probably not going to be much help, I'm afraid."

"You didn't see anything at all? Are you sure?"

"Positive. I know I shouldn't complain given what happened to that poor couple, but that trip was particularly tiresome."

"Oh? Why so?"

"Before I retired, I used to work as a literary agent. The guard, who was working in the buffet car, must have found out because he spent a good part of the journey pitching some awful novel to me. I told him that I was no longer in the business, but he was convinced I must still have connections. As it happens, I do, but I wouldn't abuse those friendships by giving out their details to everyone with a book to peddle. In the end, I had to be very blunt, and told him that these days, in order to be published, you need an angle. Unless you're a celebrity or have created some buzz in the media, you stand very little chance of landing a publishing deal. I'm not sure that's what he was hoping to hear, but it seemed to do the trick because he finally took the hint and left me alone."

"And there's nothing else about that journey that stands out?"

"Nothing, I'm afraid. I'm sorry I can't be of more help."

Thorny was a delightful old girl, but she hadn't been able to offer much help.

***

I needed to find out more about the Shores' relationship, so when I got back to the office, I went online to check out the newspapers published just after the incident. In one of The Bugle's articles, there was a quote from a woman named Angie Crawford who was described as Gena Shore's closest friend. The quote itself was unremarkable, but it struck me that this woman might be able to give me her take on the Shores' relationship. So far, all I had to go on was what the

Ganders had told me, and they were no doubt biased towards Gary. Tracking down Angie Crawford proved to be easy enough, and when I spoke to her on the phone, she agreed to meet with me the following day. I offered to go to her place, but she asked if we could meet in a coffee shop in Washbridge. I suggested Coffee Triangle. She'd never heard of it, but thought it sounded fun.

I'd just finished on the call to Angie Crawford when Jules came through to my office.

"There's a woman here to see you; her name is Deli."

Oh bum! She would no doubt be distraught over Mad's sudden departure.

"You can send her through, but before you do, how are things between you and Gilbert? I couldn't help but overhear the altercation earlier."

"I'm sorry about that, Jill; I just saw red. I feel bad now because I caught him on the side of the head with the stapler."

"Is he okay?"

"Yeah. It didn't break the skin. Anyway, we've made up now. He's promised not to mention bottle tops again, and I've promised not to give Lules a hard time about the Miss Bottle Top competition."

Deli was wearing a boob tube and a micro skirt; a vision in yellow.

"Deli. This is a surprise."

"I hope you don't mind me dropping in like this, Jill." She glanced around. "Looks like Nails did a good job."

"He certainly did. I can't thank you both enough. I suppose you're here about Mad?"

"Madeline? No. Nothing much I can do about that now. She'll be back when she needs something. The reason I popped in was to let you know that we're going to be neighbours."

"Are you moving to Smallwash?" Oh, no!

"Me and Nails live in Smallwash?" She laughed. "It's a bit too la-di-da for the likes of us. You wouldn't want us dragging down the property prices, would you?"

"Don't be silly." I breathed a silent sigh of relief.

"I meant we're going to be business neighbours."

"Oh?"

"I've just signed a sub-lease with the sweaty guys next door."

"I-Sweat? I didn't realise they were renting out space."

"They've got a few small rooms along the corridor that they aren't using. I saw their ad in The Bugle."

"What will you be doing there?"

"Nails."

"Oh, right, sorry. I didn't realise it was Nails' business. What will he be doing?"

"No." She laughed. "It isn't Nails' business; it's mine. *Nails* are what I'll be doing. I'm going to open a Nail Bar. It'll be called: Nailed It! It was Nails who came up with the name. What do you think of it?"

"It's—err—great. I didn't realise you were qualified as a nail—err—"

"Technician? Oh yes. I did a correspondence course last summer. Got a diploma and everything."

"Right. It all sounds great. When will Nailed It! be opening?"

"As soon as we've fitted it out. Nails is looking for equipment and furniture now. He reckons he knows where to pick some up second-hand. We're going to have a big launch do—you can be our first customer if you like? You'll get your picture in the paper."

"Thanks. That's a very kind offer, but I don't really go in for nail treatments. I know someone who'd love the opportunity, though."

"Who's that?"

"My sister, Kathy, loves to get her nails done. She's one of the Everettes at Ever, on the high street."

"Ever whats?"

"Haven't you seen them? You should definitely check them out, particularly if you like red trouser suits."

Snigger.

***

Deli had no sooner left than something huge and furry appeared on my window sill. It was an enormous cat, and I didn't need my detective skills to work out that it must be Big Gordy. I quickly cast a spell to hide Winky who had already scurried under the sofa.

"Can I help you?"

"Hello, darlin'." He jumped down from the window sill, and then up onto my desk.

"Do you mind?"

"Not at all. Who are you, little witchy?"

"Never mind who I am. Who are you, and what gives you the right to come strolling into my office?"

"My name is Gordon, but everyone calls me Big Gordy. Would you like to know why?"

"Definitely not."

"I'm here on a bit of unfinished business. If you could

tell me where I can find a certain Mr Winky, I'll be out of your hair in no time."

"Winky isn't here."

"I can see that, but I can smell the salmon, so he can't be very far away."

Mental note to self: renew the air fresheners. "Like I said, he isn't here. He had an accident last night."

"What kind of accident?"

"He was hit by a car. Nothing too serious, but the vet is going to keep him in for a few days."

"How tragic. I'm very sorry to hear that. Maybe you could give him a message from me."

"Okay."

"Tell him that in light of the unfortunate circumstances in which he finds himself, I'm prepared to extend our arrangement until the end of the week. But no longer."

"What *arrangement* would that be?"

"That's confidential, darlin'. I'm not at liberty to say."

"Okay, I'll tell him."

"How about you and I go for a cocktail? I know a bar not far from here."

"Thanks, but I'll have to pass. Busy, busy, busy."

"Here's my card, just in case you change your mind."

And with that, he hightailed it out of the office.

"Has he gone?" invisible Winky said.

"Yes. It's all clear." I reversed the 'hide' spell. "I assume you heard that? You have a week to come up with the money."

"I don't suppose you could lend it to me?"

"You don't suppose correctly."

Chapter 7

I'd arranged to meet Murray Murray at the colonel's old house.

"Welcome, Jill." He greeted me at the door. "It must be a while since you were last here?"

"It is," I lied. Little did he know that I'd been at the house quite recently when I'd pretended to be Lady Raybourn, while working on the Hauntings Unlimited case.

"Follow me." He led the way down a corridor, and then stopped outside a door. "Listen," he said, in a hushed voice.

I listened, but could hear nothing, so I shrugged.

"Put your ear to the door."

I did as he said, but could still hear nothing.

He beckoned me to follow him to one of the reception rooms which looked out over the beautiful gardens.

"You didn't hear anything, I take it?" he said.

"Not a thing. Should I have?"

"Lorenzo, my ghostwriter, is in there now. He's supposedly typing my novel on the manual typewriter, but I can't hear a thing."

"Maybe he's just thinking between writing sprints?"

"But there are never any sounds. I've stood outside that door for ages, and yet I've never once heard the sound of the typewriter."

"The doors in this house are very thick, maybe —"

Just then, there was a knock at the door.

"Come in," Murray shouted.

The man who entered the room was several stones overweight, and sweating profusely.

"Sorry to disturb you, Murray, but I've finished for the day." He walked over to Murray, and handed him several sheets of A4 paper.

"Thanks, Lorenzo. See you on Monday."

"Same time?"

"Yes, please."

"I take it that was your ghostwriter?" I said, after the man had left.

"Yes. I asked you over here at this time of day deliberately because I knew he'd be finished about now. Let's go back to the office."

This time, Murray took me inside the room, in the centre of which was a table and chair. On the table was a solid-looking manual typewriter; next to it was a packet of white paper.

"Will you go back out of the room, Jill, and close the door behind you? I'll type a few words to see if you can hear me."

"Okay."

Moments later, I heard the typewriter keys striking the paper, so I went back inside. "Yes, I could hear you."

"That's what I thought. And I was typing as light-fingered as I could. There's no way that he can be typing without it being heard outside."

"I don't understand what that means." I admitted.

"Neither do I, but I'm worried. I can't afford for excerpts of this manuscript to be leaked, and right now, I don't feel comfortable with what is happening here. Do you think you'll be able to get to the bottom of it?"

"Maybe. He said he would be back on Monday, didn't he?"

"That's right."

"Okay. I'll see you then."

***

I'd promised Lules that I would ask Norman if he'd tutor her on the subject of bottle tops, but there was no sign of him when I called in at Top Of The World.

"Can I help you?" A young man with slicked-back hair, and a sharp line in suits, cornered me.

"I was looking for Norman?"

"He isn't here at the moment. I'm Rory Storey. Can I help?"

"I just wanted a word with him."

"I have just the bottle top for you."

"No, thanks. I'm not a collector."

"You don't need to be a collector to appreciate this little beauty. Just look at those lines. Have you ever seen anything as beautiful as that?"

"It's just a bottle top."

"This isn't just *any* bottle top. It's the elite of bottle tops. An investment that will pay rich dividends in years to come."

"I'm really not interested."

"No problem. I completely understand. You'll probably be more interested in our budget range."

"I'm not interested in *any* bottle tops. Now, if you'd just tell me where I can find Norman."

"He's gone down to Coffee Triangle with that bird from the bookies."

What a piece of work this guy was.

I spotted Norman, sitting with Tonya in the far corner of

the coffee shop.

"Hello, you two."

Norman stared at me for a few moments before the lights came on, but then he recognised me.

"Hello, Jill. This is Tonya."

"We've already met." I smiled at her.

"I've never seen you before in my life." She stared blankly at me.

"I've been in WashBets several times recently."

"I don't remember."

"I came in to see Ryan."

"If you had a complaint, you should have seen Bryan."

"Right, okay. Anyway, Norman, I was just wondering whether you'd have the time to tutor someone on the subject of bottle tops."

"Sure. When would you like to start?"

"It isn't for me; it's for my PA, Jules, that I'm asking. Her sister is entering the Miss Bottle Top competition. As part of that contest, she has to display a knowledge of the bottle top industry. Her name is Lules."

"I thought you said it was Jules?"

"No. Jules works for me. Lules is her sister."

"What does Lules do?"

"She works at the black pudding factory, and she models part-time."

"Is she pretty?" Tonya interrupted.

"Err — well, she is currently Miss Black Pudding."

"I don't think it's a good idea, Normy," Tonya said.

"It'll be cool, Tonny babe. I only have eyes for you. You know that." He gave her a long, sloppy kiss. I averted my gaze until they came up for air.

"When would Lules want to do this?" he asked.

"Shall I tell her to get in touch with you at Top Of The World?"

"Yeah. Ask her to drop in and see me."

"Great, thanks. Bye, Norman. Bye, Tonya."

As I walked away, I heard her say, "I've no idea who she is, Normy."

***

When I pulled onto my street, there were not one, but two removal vans parked across the road from our house. Jack was in the lounge, staring out of the front window.

"It looks like both of our new neighbours are moving in," he said, without even looking at me.

"Don't I get a kiss, nosey?"

"I wasn't being nosey. I was being an interested neighbour." He gave me a quick kiss, but then went back to being nosey.

"Have you seen who's moving in?" I asked.

"Not yet."

"It didn't take the agent long to let those."

"That's hardly surprising. Haven't you seen the articles on the shortage of property to rent in and around Washbridge?"

"Let's hope that whoever it is doesn't play the bagpipes. Or have a land train."

"We should give them a cake as a welcome to the neighbourhood present," Jack suggested.

"Why?"

"Because that's the neighbourly thing to do. Why don't you bake a couple?"

"No chance. If you want to give them cake, you'd better

buy some from the corner shop."

"I will. In fact, I'll go down there now."

"I'll come with you. I could do with some fresh air. How are we for custard creams?"

"Why are you asking me? It's not like I'm allowed to eat them."

A quick check showed I was down to my last three packets, so it was definitely time to restock.

"Do we need anything else while we're there?" Jack said.

"How are we for buckets?"

"We have enough."

"Okay. Let's go do this."

When we stepped into the shop, our way was blocked by a line of string across the aisle. We had to practically limbo in order to get underneath it. After picking out a couple of nice-looking cakes, and grabbing five packets of custard creams, we made our way to the counter. Little Jack Corner seemed to have abandoned his hydraulic platform, and had reverted to the more basic, but much safer, wooden box.

"Hello, you two. Cakes? Is it a birthday?"

"No," Jack said. "These are for our new neighbours."

"What a very nice gesture. And the biscuits? Are you inviting them around for a cup of tea?"

"No, they're all for Jill."

"They do have to last me for quite a while," I offered in my defence. "By the way, did you know there's a length of string running across the aisles?"

"That's my new invention." He picked up a tin can that was attached to the length of string. "Missy? Come in. Do you copy?"

A weak voice came back, "I copy, Jack."

"See," he said, proudly. "Before, when we were at opposite ends of the shop, we weren't able to communicate, but now, with this, it's no problem."

"That's fantastic," I said, with as much enthusiasm as I could muster.

"Missy is near to the buckets. Would you like me to ask her to bring you one?"

Before I could answer, there was a loud crash on the road outside.

Jack rushed for the door; I was a couple of steps behind him. Fortunately, we both remembered to duck under the string. The scene that met us was horrific. A car had left the road and ploughed straight into a lamppost. The front-end was crumpled, and the driver looked in a bad way. Standing next to the wrecked vehicle was a familiar face.

"Lester?"

He looked up, and nodded to me. "He's gone, Jill. Dead."

Jack started towards the vehicle, but I grabbed his arm. "It's too late, Jack. There's nothing you can do."

"Is Lester a doctor?"

"Err—no, but he's medically trained."

"I should at least call the police and ambulance, just in case."

"Yeah. You do that while I have a quick word with Lester."

While Jack was on the phone to the emergency services, I hurried across to Lester.

"Are you sure he's dead?"

"Positive. Luckily I was only just down the street."

"Not so lucky for him. What happens now?"

"It'll only take me a few moments to process him, and then I'll be on my way."

"I do wish there was a better term than 'process'."

"Sorry. This is my first assignment since I qualified, so I'm a little nervous."

"The emergency services are on their way." Jack had now joined us. "Is there anything else I can do, Lester?"

"No. I've got this. I'll stay here until the emergency services arrive."

"Come on, Jack." I grabbed his arm. "We should go."

"Shouldn't we wait here with Lester?"

"No need." Lester waved away the offer. "I'm fine."

"You and Lucy should come around for dinner sometime," Jack said.

"Sure. Or you and Jill could come to us?"

Come to us? What was Lester thinking? How was Jack meant to visit the sup world?

"He's a nice guy," Jack said, as we made our way back to the house. "We should definitely all have dinner sometime."

"Yeah, but it would have to be at our place. I didn't like to say anything in front of Lester, but Aunt Lucy is the world's worst cook."

"Tell me again what it is that Lester does for a living."

"He's a — err — despatch clerk."

Chapter 8

Even though I was snowed under with work, I was still determined to somehow track down the descendants of Helen Drewmore. I was now convinced that they were the key to my discovering more information about what I'd seen in that small room at CASS. I had to find the identities of the two people whose portraits were in my locket, and work out what connection, if any, they had to me. The only problem was, I didn't know where to start.

But I knew someone who might.

I magicked myself over to Aunt Lucy's.

"Jill, I was going to give you a call later. Lester told me that you and Jack saw him last night. I'm sorry I didn't get the chance to tell you that he'd been allocated to the Smallwash area. I only found out myself yesterday."

"That's okay. It was a bit awkward, though. He was—err—processing a client at the time."

"Oh dear."

"That wasn't the worst of it. Jack suggested that the four of us should have dinner sometime."

"That's not so terrible, is it?"

"Of course not, but Lester said we could come to you."

"He said *what*?"

"It must have been the pressure of dealing with his first client. I think I managed to talk my way out of it, though. I told Jack we shouldn't come here because you were such a terrible cook."

She laughed. "It's a good thing you had your wits about you. I'll have words with Lester."

"Don't be too hard on him. I suspect he's feeling pretty stressed now that he's out on his own."

"Would you like a cup of tea?"

"Not just now, I have to go and see a troll in a few minutes. I popped in because I was hoping I might pick your brain."

"Slim pickings to be found there, but I'll help if I can."

"I was wondering what's the best way of tracing a family tree in Candlefield? It's relatively simple in the human world because I have the internet to rely on, but I'm struggling a bit in the sup world."

"Who are you trying to trace?"

"I—err—no one in particular. It's just something that would be handy to know for when I'm working cases over here."

"Right." She didn't sound convinced, but as I'd hoped, she didn't press me. "Your best bet would probably be the Candlefield Electoral Society. Their offices are based in the town hall, I believe."

"I should have thought of that. Thanks." I turned to leave, but then I had an idea. "I don't suppose I could borrow your car, could I?"

"Of course. I hardly ever use it. I'll give you my spare key, and then you can take it anytime you like."

"Thanks."

***

I drove to the bridge where Cole the troll worked. After parking in a nearby layby, I made my way across the bridge on foot. I was almost half-way across when something jumped up from underneath it, blocking my way.

"Give me money!" the troll demanded.

"No."

"But you have to give me money if you want to cross the bridge."

"I don't think so."

"But you have to. This is a troll bridge."

"That's very good." I laughed. "Are you Cole?"

"How did you know?"

"Your cousin, Timothy, asked me to pay you a visit."

"Are you the witch detective?"

"I guess I am."

"Sorry, I didn't realise. Would you like to go under the bridge to talk?"

"Is it muddy down there?"

"It is a little."

"Why don't we stay up here, then?"

"Okay. The reason I wanted to talk to you is I think someone must be stealing my customers."

"How do you mean?"

"I've been under this same bridge for several years now. Every day, dozens upon dozens of people used to come across here. That netted me a nice income. But then, suddenly, a few months ago, most of the people stopped coming. Instead of getting dozens of customers, I'm now lucky to get two or three in a day. How am I supposed to live on that? I need you to find out what has happened to my customers—to find out who is stealing them."

"I don't really understand how anyone could 'steal' your customers unless they'd blockaded the road or set up a diversion, but I've just driven here, and I saw nothing like that."

"Something must have happened, and it's left me practically penniless. Please, will you help me?"

"If you're penniless, how are you going to pay me for my time?"

"I can't." His bottom lip quivered, and for a moment, I thought he was going to cry.

"Look, I can't promise anything, but I'll see if I can work out what's caused this problem, and if I do, I'll let you know."

"Thank you so much." He threw his arms around me, and gave me a hug.

Let me tell you: being hugged by a troll is not my favourite thing in the world.

***

After saying goodbye to Cole, I drove very slowly back the way I'd come. I wanted to make absolutely sure that there was nothing obvious that might be stopping travellers (or customers, as Cole referred to them) making their way to the bridge. I got all the way back to the main road without spotting anything, but then it occurred to me that maybe the road sign had been removed. I drove back along the main road to check, but there it was—clearly signposted to 'North Candle'.

I felt bad for Cole, but there wasn't much else I could do. He would just have to find himself another bridge, or maybe transfer to a well.

I needed coffee and a muffin. All that driving up and down the road had taken its *troll* on me.

Troll? Get it? Come on—this is some of my best material.

Pearl was back in Cuppy C today. Both she and Amber

were behind the counter.

"Where did you skive off to yesterday?" I asked Pearl.

"You're wasting your time, Jill." Amber huffed. "She won't tell."

"That's because it's none of your business." Pearl turned on her sister.

"It is when you leave me in the lurch."

"Girls! Girls! I'm sorry I mentioned it."

Once I had my drink and muffin, I went to sit by the window. Moments later, Pearl pulled up the chair next to mine.

"Sorry about just now," she said.

"That's okay. I was only poking fun; it's none of my business where you went."

"I went to see the doctor."

"Are you okay?"

"I'm great. Look, you mustn't tell Amber or Mum, but I—err—I probably shouldn't say anything."

I was getting a very strong sense of déjà vu.

"You're pregnant."

"How did you know?"

"Amber!" I called. "Come over here, would you?"

Pearl looked horrified. "You mustn't tell her!"

"What's going on?" Amber said.

"Pull up a chair."

"Jill! Don't!" Pearl pleaded.

"Pearl, you're going to be an auntie."

"Jill!" Amber looked daggers at me.

"Amber, you're going to be an auntie, too."

"What?" They echoed.

"You're—?" Amber looked at her sister.

Pearl nodded. "You too?"

The two of them hugged, and we all cried.

A few minutes later, after we'd all managed to compose ourselves, I stood up, and said, "Come on then."

"Where?"

"You have to tell Aunt Lucy."

"No!" Amber looked horrified.

"I can't." So did Pearl.

"You have to. It's not fair to expect me to keep this secret from your mother. If you didn't want her to know, then you shouldn't have told me."

"You have to come with us," Pearl said.

"Okay. I've got Aunt Lucy's car outside. Jump in—there's no time like the present."

On the way over to Aunt Lucy's house, neither of the twins spoke.

"I think I'm going to be sick," Pearl said, as we reached the door.

"Don't worry. It'll be good practice for the weeks to come." I led the way inside.

"Hello, you three." Aunt Lucy greeted us. "What's going on?"

"The twins have something to tell you."

"Oh?"

Amber looked at Pearl. Pearl looked at Amber. Neither of them spoke.

"You're pregnant, aren't you?" Aunt Lucy beamed.

"How did you know?" Amber said.

"A mother knows. Come here both of you. Give me a hug."

***

Much to my chagrin, it was triangle day in Coffee Triangle. I would have suggested we relocate to a different coffee shop, but Angie Crawford had already bought her coffee by the time I arrived.

"This place is something else." She struck her triangle. "Do you come here often?"

"Quite often, but I usually try to avoid triangle day."

"Why's that?"

"No reason. It's just that I prefer the tambourine. Or maracas."

"I'm actually quite partial to a triangle." She struck it again, just to prove the point.

"Thanks for agreeing to see me at such short notice."

"No problem. Are you working with the police?"

"Sort of, but I was actually hired by Lucy Gander."

"Gena's sister-in-law?"

"You know her?"

"No, but Gena has mentioned her a few times. From what I can gather, Lucy and her brother were very close."

"I'm hoping you'll be able to throw some light on the state of Gena and Gary's relationship. Lucy seems to think they had a good marriage."

Angie shook her head. "Then she must have been blind. Or stupid."

"Are you saying things weren't good between Gary and Gena?"

"Gena was going to leave him."

"Did Gary know?"

"He knew she wasn't happy, but he had no idea that she planned to leave. She was going to tell him on the day she was murdered."

"She told you that?"

"Yes. I tried to talk her out of it, but she was determined."

"Wasn't that the day of their anniversary?"

"Yes. Gary had booked the train trip weeks before. Gena said she wanted to tell him that she was leaving while they were in a public place. She was afraid how he might react if they were somewhere by themselves. I told her it was a bad idea—that it was cruel to do it on their anniversary, but she was determined."

"Was she seeing someone else?"

"Yeah. His name is Don Preston; she met him six months ago."

"Did Gary know about the other man?"

"Cripes, no. That would have totally destroyed him. Gena was his whole life."

"Do you think Gary killed her?"

She nodded. "He must have seen red when she told him she was leaving." Angie began to well up. "I'm sorry. I still can't believe she's gone. We'd known each other since we were kids. I don't even have a recent photo to remember her by."

"I have one that you can have."

"Really?"

"If you want it, that is. Gary asked one of the other passengers to take a photo of them when they first got on the train. But of course, they're both on it."

"That's okay. I can cut that pig out of it."

"I took out my phone, and brought up the photograph. "This is it. I'll email it to you if you're sure you want it."

Angie didn't answer. Instead, she just stared at the screen.

"I'm sorry. I didn't mean for it to upset you."

"That's Don." She pointed at the photo.

"Sorry?"

"He's the man that Gena was seeing." She touched her finger to the screen. "There, in the seat behind them. That's Don Preston."

"Are you sure?"

"Yeah. That's him."

"Did Gena tell you he was going to be on the train?"

"No. I don't think she can have known he'd planned to be there."

"Do you know where Don lives?"

"No, but I know where he works. Do you know the phone shop next door to the indoor market?"

"I don't, but I'll find it." I stood up.

"Shouldn't we tell the police about Don?"

"Probably. Finish your coffee first, and then give them a call, would you?"

I sprinted over to the indoor market.

What? Okay, it wasn't so much a sprint as a brisk walk.

Top Phone was a small independent shop. It was almost impossible to see through the window because of the posters, offering 'exclusive deals', that were plastered all over the glass.

Inside, two customers were standing at the counter. A young woman, wearing a turquoise T-shirt with the words 'Top Phone' on the front, was obviously struggling to show them how to do something. At the back of the shop was a man, wearing an identical T-shirt. It was the man from the photograph.

"Can I help you?" He approached me, all beard and

teeth.

"We need to talk in the back." I grabbed him by the arm, and frogmarched him towards the door marked: Staff Only.

"You can't come in here."

"Be quiet and listen. We don't have long before the police arrive."

"Police?"

"I know you were on the Washbridge Flyer the day that Gena and Gary Shore were murdered."

The colour drained from his face. "He killed Gena. There wasn't anything I could do."

"And then you killed him?"

"No. He'd already jumped off the train when I got there. Honestly."

"It isn't me you need to convince; it's the police. But if you are innocent, you'd better tell me everything you know before they get here."

"Who are you?"

"I'm your one and only hope, so you'd better tell me what happened."

"I begged Gena not to go on the trip, but she thought that by breaking the news to her husband on the train he'd be less likely to react violently. I wasn't so sure — that's why I booked a ticket too. I wanted to be there for her in case things turned nasty." His head dropped. "I failed her."

"What happened in the carriage?"

"Gena saw me as soon as they got on the train. She shot me such a look, but she didn't say anything to Gary. The poor guy had pulled out all the stops. He'd bought champagne, chocolates and flowers. He had no idea what she was about to do. When I caught her eye, I shook my head—I was trying to tell her not to go through with it, but she took no notice. She should have left it for another time. I could tell when she'd broken the news to him because he started screaming at her. Everyone in the carriage was staring at them. Gena dashed to the toilet, and Gary went after her. I should have followed straightaway, but I waited. I figured they'd be having a slanging match in the corridor. When they didn't come back, I went to see what was happening. That's when I found her."

"Was she still alive?"

"I don't think so. There was so much blood."

"What about the knife?"

"I never saw it."

"Are you sure?"

"Yes. It wasn't there."

"And Gary?"

"He'd gone too. The door was still swinging open."

Just then, there was a commotion out in the shop.

"Don Porter!" A female voice shouted. It was Sue Shay.

"That's the police," I said. "You'd better come with me." I led the way back into the shop.

Sushi was flanked by two uniformed police officers. When she saw me, her face flushed red. "What are you doing here, Gooder?"

"I was thinking of upgrading my phone."

She looked as though she wanted to kill me, but turned her attention to Preston. "Don Preston, I'd like you to accompany me to the station."

"Why? I haven't done anything."

"We have a few questions that we need you to answer."

"I want a lawyer."

"Of course. We can sort that out once we're at the station."

While Sushi was distracted with Preston, I slid quietly away.

Chapter 9

It was Saturday, and we were on our way to visit Jack's parents. We'd taken his car, and although I'd offered to share the driving, he'd said he was happy to do it all. Naturally, Jack was looking forward to seeing his mum and dad, and so was I, but I wasn't looking forward to the conversation that I needed to have with Yvonne. According to Grandma's sources, the new chief witchfinder was determined to make his mark by destroying me. He'd apparently put two or three of his top witchfinders on the job. I was hoping that Yvonne would know something about it, and that she might be able to help me to identify my adversaries. There was, of course, no guarantee that the trip would yield the result I hoped for. Yvonne had retired, so she might no longer be in the loop. Even if she did know about the change at the top, she might not know the identity of the witchfinders who had been set on my trail. There was one other possibility — one that I didn't like to think about, but was forced to consider: She might have the information I needed, but be unwilling to share it with me. The witchfinders were her people, so passing that information to me would be a betrayal. Although Jack was the most important thing in her life, there might still be lines she was not prepared to cross.

We'd been driving for just under an hour when Jack pushed a CD into the player.

"What's that awful noise?" I complained.

"This isn't *noise*. It's a big band compilation."

"Can't we listen to some soul?"

"I need to get into the mood in preparation for the big

competition next Saturday. You haven't forgotten about it, have you?"

"I've tried to, believe me. I hate this music. It's just a lot of men blowing trumpets."

"You really don't have a musical gene in your body, do you?"

"Says you. Anyway, you'd better make sure Mrs V and Armi win."

"You're surely not suggesting I show them any favouritism?"

"I'm not suggesting it; I'm outright saying it. Mrs V would love it if they won."

"No one wants to win by cheating."

Hmm?

By the time we arrived at his parents' house, I'd had enough of Jack's big band music to last me a lifetime. There's only so much saxophone a person can take.

"Hi, Mum." Jack gave her a kiss.

His dad gave me a welcoming hug.

"It's lovely to see you both again so soon." Yvonne led the way inside.

"Like I mentioned on the phone," Jack said. "It was Jill's idea that we should visit."

"We're delighted to have you both. Are you sure you can only stay the one night? You're welcome to stay for as long as you like."

"We both have work on Monday, Mum."

"Of course." Yvonne smiled. "I forget that people have to go to work. I've put you in the back room, Jack. Jill, you're in the front next to us."

Jack and I exchanged a glance.

"Just kidding." Yvonne laughed. "You're both in the back bedroom. Why don't you unpack, splash your faces, and then join us in the lounge? Roy has bought a bottle of bubbly for us to celebrate your visit."

"You shouldn't have gone to all that expense," I said.

"Nonsense. Besides, it's only the cheap stuff."

After we'd unpacked, which didn't take more than a few minutes, we both freshened up, and then went downstairs where Yvonne and Roy were waiting in the lounge.

"To health and happiness!" Roy proposed the toast.

"Health and happiness!" We all echoed.

We made small talk for the next hour, but then Yvonne excused herself to go and prepare dinner. I offered to help, but she wouldn't hear of it. I wasn't sure if she didn't want to impose, or if Jack had told her about my culinary skills — or the lack thereof.

Roy showed us around the garden, which was truly magnificent, and thankfully devoid of gnomes.

"We've just had a sandpit put in," Jack said.

"Really? Why?"

"Jill thought it would be nice for the kids."

Roy turned to me. "Are you —?"

"Goodness, no. Jack's talking about my niece and nephew. Well, just my niece, really. Mikey is too old for sandpits, apparently."

"I guess it'll still be there when you two decide the time is right for kids." Roy grinned.

"Moving on," Jack jumped in. "How are the tomatoes this year?"

Yvonne was an excellent cook. She'd made roast duck with plum sauce; it looked and tasted delicious. Having been brought up eating meals like this one, it must have been something of a culture shock for Jack when he tasted my feeble offerings.

"More pudding, Jill?" Yvonne offered.

"I'd love to. It's delicious. But if I eat another mouthful, I'll explode."

"In that case, it's time for the men to do the washing up while you and I wash this down with another glass of wine."

"No, you must let Jack and me do the washing up," I insisted.

What? Of course I didn't mean it; I knew full well she wouldn't take me up on the offer. Snigger!

"I won't hear of it. Roy and Jack can talk their boring men-talk while we have an intelligent conversation."

Yvonne took my hand, led me out of the dining room, and through to the lounge. Once inside, she closed the door behind her.

"I know why you're here," she said, in a hushed voice.

"You do?"

"I assume it's about Rex Wrathbringer."

I nodded.

"I think I can help, but we can't get into it now in case we're overheard. Let's meet down here tonight—say two am?"

"Okay, thanks."

The evening was spent playing board games (I won, naturally) and chatting. Much to my delight, Yvonne managed to thoroughly embarrass Jack when she brought out photographs of him as a baby.

"You were really chubby," I teased him.

"I was not chubby."

"Look at this one of you in the bath."

"I think we've seen more than enough of these." He snatched the album from me. "I don't know about the rest of you, but I'm tuckered out. I'm going up to bed."

"Me too." I stifled a yawn.

We said our goodnights, and I followed Jack upstairs.

"Your mum and dad are great," I said, once we were tucked up in bed.

"They love you too. Or at least they did until they saw you turn into board game psycho."

"What are you talking about?"

"The games are just meant to be fun."

"I know that."

"Then why did you shout, 'You're bankrupt, loser!' to my dad when he couldn't pay the fee for landing on your hotel?"

"Were those my exact words? I don't think so. I seem to remember saying something along the lines of: jolly hard luck."

Jack was soon fast asleep, but I daren't allow myself to doze off in case I slept straight through to morning. At just before two, I slipped out of bed, and crept downstairs to find Yvonne waiting for me in the lounge.

"Close the door behind you, Jill. Roy is a light sleeper."

I did as she said, and joined her on the sofa.

"How much do you already know?" she asked.

"Only what Grandma has told me."

"Your grandmother? How has she heard about any of

this?"

"There isn't much Grandma doesn't know. For example, she knows you're a witchfinder."

"What?" Yvonne looked shocked. "How?"

"She said that she sensed it as soon as you two met."

"Oh dear. What exactly did she tell you about Rex Wrathbringer?"

"That he'd recently been appointed head of the witchfinders, and that he wanted to make his mark by destroying some high-profile witches."

"It's much more specific than that. He has his sights firmly set on you, and you alone. He knows that if he succeeds in destroying you, it will be a big feather in his cap."

"Do you know him?"

"Rex? Oh, yes. I knew him when he was a Radish." She grinned. "He's a horrible little man who should never have risen to such a high office, but then he always did know how to play politics. The good news is that I have information which may help you."

"That's good to hear. I wasn't sure if you would—what with being retired."

"I still have a few contacts at head office."

"If you help me, won't that get back to your contacts?"

"It's possible, but that's a risk I'm willing to take. I hate the idea of betraying colleagues I've known for decades, but my first loyalty always has been, and always will be to my family. And I now consider you to be part of my family."

"Thank you." I gave her a hug, and somehow managed to hold back the tears.

"I don't know how useful the information I have will

be, but it's all I've been able to obtain to-date."

"Anything you can tell me will help."

"Rex has tasked three of the most experienced, successful witchfinders with finding and destroying you. Two of them work together—they're actually twin brother and sister. Their names are Vinnie and Minnie Dreadmore. They're only in their twenties, but both have grey hair."

"They don't sound scary." I shuddered. "At all."

"They're young, but very experienced. And completely ruthless. The third one, I know very little about. He or she goes by the name of The Rose. I can't find anyone who knows anything about them, but their record speaks for itself. Over one hundred witches destroyed."

"A hundred?"

"At the last count. Almost twice as many as the next in the 'kill' league."

"That would be impressive if it wasn't so terrifying."

"You'll need to be extra vigilant, Jill. I'll try and find more information about The Rose, and if I do, I'll get a message to you somehow."

"Thanks, Yvonne, I really—"

"So, that's where you are." Jack appeared in the doorway. "I woke up and you'd gone. What are you two plotting down here?"

"I've just asked your mother to get me a huge print of your baby-in-the-bath photo so I can get it framed, and hang it in the lounge."

The next morning, Yvonne and Roy took us to their favourite country park. The weather was beautiful, and we spent over two hours just walking around, admiring the scenery. After a delicious pub lunch, it was time for Jack and me to head back to Washbridge.

"You'll have to drive." Jack handed me the car keys. "I've had a drink."

"Okay." I'd only had soda water and lime.

"Don't be strangers." Yvonne gave first me, and then Jack a big hug. Roy did likewise.

"What were you and Mum really talking about in the middle of the night?"

"None of your business."

"Were you talking about me?"

"No. Nothing so boring."

"You aren't going to tell me, are you?"

"If you must know, we were discussing witches."

"I only asked. No need to be so sarky." He reached for the CD player.

"You're not playing that awful big band noise again."

"I have to. It will help me to get into the right frame of mind for Saturday."

Rather than argue, I cast the 'sleep' spell, and then slid the Best of Soul CD into the slot.

Now that's what I call music.

Chapter 10

I had that Monday morning feeling. Why couldn't the weekend last longer? Was three days too much to ask for?

"You and mum really seemed to hit it off this weekend," Jack said, over breakfast.

"I really like Yvonne. I like your dad too, but your mum and I seem to have some kind of connection."

"That's exactly what Dad said."

"He did?"

"Yeah. He and I were talking while we were doing the washing up. He said that Mum had always felt like a bit of an outsider. I must admit it had never occurred to me. He said you were the first person that he ever felt 'got' Mum."

"That was nice of him to say."

"You and Mum seemed to have a lot of whispered conversations. What were they about?"

"You, of course. We were discussing your many faults." I kissed him. "Only kidding."

"We really should take those cakes to the new neighbours before they go stale."

"Now? They'll probably still be in bed."

"It's just turned eight; they should be up by now. You grab one and I'll take the other."

We started at what had previously been Blake and Jen's house. As soon as Jack pressed the doorbell, I could hear movement inside.

"I told you they'd be up," Jack said.

Moments later, a frail old lady, dressed in a housecoat and crumpled tights, answered the door.

"Hello?" She was shouting, which made me think she must be hard of hearing.

"Hello, there." Jack smiled. "We're from across the road."

"Pardon?"

"We're your neighbours from across the road," I shouted. "I'm Jill, and this is Jack."

"Like the nursery rhyme?"

"Err—yeah."

"Nice to meet you both. I'm Doris, but everyone calls me Blossom."

"We've brought you a cake, Blossom." I held out the box. "It's a welcome to the neighbourhood."

"How very kind. Won't you come in for a cup of tea?"

"We have to get to work."

"Just for a few minutes. It's the least I can do after you've brought me a cake."

"Okay, then, but just a quick drink."

Blake and Jen had left the majority of their furniture behind, so the house looked pretty much the same as the last time we'd been there. Jack and I sat in the lounge while Blossom made the tea.

"I'm afraid I don't have any biscuits. I haven't had chance to go to the shops yet." Blossom handed us our cups; her hands were shaking a little, but not enough to spill the tea.

"That's okay," Jack said. "There's a handy shop just down the road; on the corner."

"They have a particularly fine range of buckets," I added.

"Will you be living here alone, Blossom?" Jack said, and then took a sip of tea.

"Yes. It's just me now. Bobby and I were together for fifty-two years. He died three months ago."

"I'm sorry to hear that." I tried the tea, but it was way too sweet. She'd obviously misheard or misunderstood my sugar requirements. "Won't this house be rather big for you all alone?"

"Much too big, but I moved up here to be close to my daughter. They don't have room for me at her house — what with the children, the dogs and the parakeet. I'm only renting this until I find somewhere more suitable. A small bungalow would be ideal."

We made polite, if very loud, conversation for another ten minutes, and then I stood up.

"We'd better get going. We have another cake to deliver next door."

"Didn't you like the tea, dearie?"

"It was lovely, but I have a long drive ahead of me."

"Weak bladder, eh? Comes to us all, dearie."

"What are you smirking at?" I asked Jack, as we made our way next door.

"How's that weak bladder of yours?"

"Shut it, or you'll have a weak bladder, after I've kicked you where it hurts."

The doorbell at Mr Kilbride's old house wasn't working, so Jack knocked on the door.

"I can hear someone," he said.

No one answered, so he knocked louder.

Once again, there was the sound of movement inside, but still no one came to the door.

"Maybe they're not dressed yet," Jack said. "Come on,

we can try again after work."

Just then, the door opened a crack, and a man peered around it. For reasons known only to him, he was wearing a balaclava.

"What do you want?"

"We're from across the road. We—"

"We're very busy."

"We brought you this cake." Jack held out the box. "It's a welcome—"

"Thanks." The man snatched the box from Jack's hands, and then slammed the door shut.

"How rude!" I shook my head in disbelief.

"Maybe we just called at a bad time."

Jack—ever the diplomat.

***

As I walked from my car to the office, the headline on The Bugle caught my eye:

Death Train

I called in at the newsagent, bought a copy, and quickly skimmed the lead article. It seemed there had been another murder on the Washbridge Flyer. It was the first I'd heard of it, but then Jack and I had been travelling back from his parents' house on Sunday. According to The Bugle's sources, which granted weren't always reliable, a woman named Carol Strand had been found murdered in the corridor, close to the toilet. She had been stabbed.

This changed everything.

When I arrived at work, Desmond Sidings was seated in

the outer office.

"This gentleman doesn't have an appointment, but he insisted on waiting to see you," Jules said.

"That's okay. Would you like to come through to my office, Desmond?"

"I assume you've seen the news, Jill?"

"Yes, just now. I was away yesterday."

"This could sound the death knell for the Washbridge Flyer. No one will want to travel on a train that is being stalked by a serial killer."

"Serial killer? Isn't that a bit premature? What makes you think the same person committed the latest murder?"

"It wasn't in the news reports, but the murder weapon was found this time. The police have confirmed it's the same knife that was used to kill Gena Shore."

"That certainly blows a hole in the theory that Gary Shore murdered his wife. It probably also means that Don Preston didn't kill Gary Shore."

"Who is Don Preston?"

"Gena Shore was having an affair with him. It turns out he was on the first trip too."

"I had no idea."

"Neither did the police until Friday. He was taken in for questioning about Gary's death, but I suspect this latest incident means he will have been cleared from their enquiries."

"I have no faith in the police based on what they've done so far. Are you still working on the case?"

"I am, but there's a good chance the Ganders may no longer require my services after the events of yesterday."

"Either way, I'd like you to stay on the case, and report to me. Would you do that? Obviously, I'll pay you for your time."

"I don't see why not."

"Great." Sidings stood up, and shook my hand. "We need to find the killer quickly or The Flyer will go out of business."

What a result! I was now being paid twice for working on the same case.

"What are you looking so pleased about?" Winky appeared from under the sofa. He was pushing a roll of tin foil ahead of him.

"I'm getting paid twice for working on the same job."

"I'm still amazed that you get paid at all."

"Less of the cheek. What's with the roll of tin foil?"

"This is my get-out-of jail card with Big Gordy."

"How is that going to save you?"

"All will become clear in time." He tore off a length of the foil.

Even though I had tons of work to do, I was fascinated to see what he was up to. Winky spent the next couple of minutes, folding the foil into shape. When he'd finished, he placed it onto his head.

"A hat? I don't get it."

"Surely, it isn't that difficult to understand, even for you. It's a tin foil hat."

"I can see that. Don't a few crazy people think that those hats will save them from aliens? I don't think anyone believes they'll work against mobster cats."

"This is just the first of many."

"Wearing more than one won't make any difference."

"They aren't for me to wear. I intend to sell them. The proceeds from the sales will give me the cash I need to pay back Big Gordy."

"You know that saying: clutching at straws? I think that must have been coined by someone in a similar situation to this. There's one major flaw with this plan of yours."

"Pray tell."

"No one, repeat no one, is going to buy your tin foil hats."

"We'll see."

***

As arranged, I got to Murray Murray's house a few minutes before Lorenzo Woolshape was due to arrive.

"I'm not sure I understand what you have planned, Jill?" Murray said.

"I'm going to hide in the room where Lorenzo will be writing. That way, I'll be able to see exactly what's going on in there."

"But there's nowhere to hide in that room. The only furniture in there is the table and chair where he'll be working."

"You forget that I do this for a living. I can guarantee he won't know I'm in the room with him."

"Okay. If you're sure." He looked far from convinced.

"I am. You show him in, and as soon as he's in the room, I need you to leave the house. Don't come back until I phone you."

"What about when he's finished the chapter? He'll expect to hand it over to me."

"Let me worry about that."

I left a very sceptical Murray in the main hall while I

made my way to the writing room. Once inside, I made myself invisible, and then waited. Ten minutes later, Murray showed Lorenzo into the room. The expression on Murray's face was a picture, as he tried to work out where I'd *hidden*.

Once Murray had left, Lorenzo walked casually around the room a couple of times, and then took a seat at the desk. But, instead of starting to type, he put his feet up onto the desk, and leaned back in the chair. Five minutes later, he was sound asleep.

I didn't get it.

Lorenzo was still fast asleep two hours later when I suddenly became aware of a sharp drop in temperature. That could mean only one thing: a ghost. Had the colonel or Priscilla decided to drop in on me?

It was neither of them. The man who appeared was slim, bordering on skinny. His stubble was more blunt-razor than designer.

"Lorenzo!" He nudged the sleeping so-called writer. "Wake up!"

"What?" Lorenzo sat up in the chair. "I must have nodded off for a couple of minutes."

A couple of minutes? He'd been out like a light for two hours.

"There you are." The ghost handed over several type-written pages.

"Good man. Same time tomorrow?"

"Of course." The ghost disappeared.

Lorenzo flicked through the pages, and nodded his approval. Then, after checking his watch, he made his way out of the room. I waited a couple of minutes, then hurried to the main hall and reversed the 'invisible' spell.

"Mr Murray had to go out," I said.

"Oh?"

"He said you were to let me have today's chapter."

"Who are you?"

"Charlotte Charlotte. I'm Murray Murray's PA."

"Charlotte Charlotte?"

"That's right. Now, if you wouldn't mind?" I held out my hand.

He handed over the pages. "Shall I wait until Murray Murray comes back?"

"There's no need. I'll see he gets these. He asked me to confirm that you'll be here the same time tomorrow?"

"Yes, of course."

"In that case, I'll bid you farewell."

"Goodbye." Still a little confused, Lorenzo left.

I now knew why Murray had heard no sounds coming from the writing room. Lorenzo had obviously employed a 'real' ghost to write the book for him. The ghost did all the work while lazy Lorenzo snoozed. Not a bad little gig! What was I supposed to tell Murray? I could hardly tell him the truth. Instead, I phoned him, and told him that so far, I'd seen nothing untoward take place. Before he could bombard me with questions, I cut short the call with the excuse that I had another, urgent appointment to keep.

Chapter 11

I magicked myself over to Aunt Lucy's house because I wanted to check how she felt about the twins' big news.

"Would you like a drink, Jill?"

"A cup of tea would go down a treat. The main reason I came over was to check on how you're doing?"

"Me? I'm fine. Why?"

"I wondered how you felt about the twins' news, now that it's had time to sink in?"

"I couldn't be happier. I can't wait to be a grandma. Speaking of which, your grandmother isn't very thrilled about the news."

"Why ever not?"

"She says she can't bear the thought of being a great-grandmother. She doesn't mean it really. Deep down, she's just as excited as I am."

"Deep down?"

"Very deep."

"By the way, thanks for letting me borrow the car the other day."

"No problem. Did you go anywhere nice?"

"Not far. Just on the road to North Candle."

"We used to go there quite often when the twins were kids. They loved the North Candle fun park. I heard that it closed down a few months back. Such a shame."

"Hold on. Are you saying that road used to be the main route to the funfair?"

"It was the only way there. It used to get really busy at peak times. The funfair was essentially the only thing in North Candle. It must be like a ghost town there now."

"Don't bother with the tea, Aunt Lucy. Could I borrow

the car again?"

"Of course. Where are you going this time?"

"I'm off to see a troll."

***

As on my previous visit, I parked in the layby, and then walked over the bridge. And just as before, Cole jumped out and demanded money.

"It's me. I came to see you last week."

"Sorry. I haven't made any money yet today, and I thought you were my first customer."

"I'm afraid not, but I think I've discovered why there are far fewer people travelling this way."

"Is someone stealing them? Have they blocked the road?"

"Nothing like that. Apparently, there used to be a popular funfair further down this road, but that's now closed down, so there's very little reason for anyone to travel this way, unless they happen to live in North Candle."

"Oh dear." He sat down on the bridge. "I suppose that means my customers will never come back?"

"It kind of looks that way. Why don't you relocate to a different bridge? One with more — err — customers?"

"That's easier said than done. There are more trolls than there are bridges to go around. I had to wait ages to get this one."

"What about a well?"

"Sorry?"

"Why don't you find yourself a well, like Timothy?"

"I'm a bridge troll. I wouldn't know what to do in a

well. You don't know very much about trolls, do you?"

"Apparently not. Surely, there must be a bridge somewhere in Candlefield that hasn't already been claimed?"

"The only way to find out would be to check the Troll Register."

"Why don't you do that, then?"

"It's held in Troll House in the centre of Candlefield. I don't like the city—it scares me."

Oh boy!

"What if I was to take you there?"

"It's appointments only. Do you have a phone?"

"Yes, why?"

"I could call them to see if they have any appointments today."

"Okay." I handed over my phone, and waited while he made the call.

"They have a cancellation in an hour's time. Shall I tell them to reserve it for me?"

"Yes, go ahead."

***

When we arrived in Candlefield, Cole took hold of my arm. He was obviously very nervous, which wasn't altogether surprising because you didn't see many trolls in the city centre.

I checked my watch. "We've got thirty minutes to kill. My cousins have a tea room not far from here. We could get something to eat and drink there while we wait."

"Timothy is always banging on about a place he goes to, called Coffee Trolley. Do you think we could go there instead?"

"I guess so. I can't say I've ever seen it. Where is it exactly?"

"On PidgeonToe Road."

"Okay. That's this way, if my memory serves me right."

When we reached the coffee shop, I hesitated at the door. "Are you sure I'm okay to go in here?"

"Why wouldn't you be?"

"Everyone in there is a troll."

"It's very popular with trolls, but anyone is allowed in."

"Are you sure?"

"Positive. Timothy told me all about it."

Despite Cole's reassurances, I still felt rather out of place, and it was obvious from the looks that I attracted, that they didn't see many other sups in there. Still, I have to admit that those trolls made a mean cup of coffee, and the muffins were to die for.

We arrived at Troll House with five minutes to spare. Cole tried to get me to go inside with him, but I insisted that this was something he needed to do for himself. I waited on the steps outside, and amused myself by counting the number of wizards who walked by, wearing toupees. What can I tell you? I'm easily amused.

Twenty minutes later, when Cole re-emerged, I could tell it wasn't good news.

"What happened?"

"There are no other bridges free. All they could do was put me on the waiting list."

"Did they give you any idea how long you might be on there?"

"No. They just said I should expect a long wait. What am I supposed to do? I can't live on what I'm making at the moment."

Although I felt really sorry for Cole, there was nothing I could do to help, so I drove him back to his bridge, and wished him luck.

* * *

I'd promised to update Grandma on my trip to see Yvonne, so after magicking myself back to Washbridge, I called in at Ever. On arrival, I spotted two new Everettes busy at work. There was barely a free seat in the tea room; that would please Grandma.

She was in her office, poking her teeth with a toothpick.

"I see you've recruited some more Everettes."

"It was the only way to get that sister of yours to stop complaining."

"Do you have to do that with your teeth?"

"I've got a piece of cashew stuck. There! That's got it!"

"Great."

"What's the skinny on the witchfinders?"

"You were right about Rex Wrathbringer."

"Of course I was right. You didn't need to go all the way up there just to confirm that."

"If I could finish? Yvonne reckons that three of the top witchfinders have been tasked with taking me out."

"What about me?"

"Yvonne seemed to think they were only interested in getting me. Anyway, as I was saying, there are three of them. She knew who two of them were: a pair who always work together. They're brother and sister: Vinnie and Minnie Dreadmore. According to Yvonne, they have the highest kill-rate of all witchfinders except for one."

"Did she give you a description?"

"They're young—in their twenties, but they both have grey hair."

"What about the third one?"

"They're known only as The Rose. No one knows who he or she is, but they have the highest kill rate of all time."

"It's not much to go on."

"It's everything Yvonne knows. She's taken a massive risk in passing this information on to me. Not only is she betraying her former colleagues, but she's also putting herself in danger."

"Very noble, I'm sure. Have you seen anyone who fits the description of the brother and sister act?"

"No."

"You should go and stay in Candlefield; it would be safer there."

"No chance. TDO couldn't drive me out of Washbridge, and neither will these witchfinders."

"Just be careful. You know where I am if you need me."

"Thanks, Grandma." I turned to leave.

"Hold on. I wanted a quick word about Saturday."

"What's happening on Saturday?"

"It's the ballroom dancing competition, of course."

"How could I forget?"

"I'm going to need you to help on the day."

"Doing what?"

"Organising the contestants, and looking after the judges. That kind of thing."

"Why not? Seeing as Jack's going to be here anyway. Was that all you wanted?"

"Just one more thing."

"Yes?"

"Be careful out there."

As I made my way up the high street, I spotted two familiar faces seated next to the window in Coffee Triangle. Norman and Lules were deep in conversation, and seemed to be getting on famously. Norman said something, and Lules cracked up with laughter. Who knew that bottle tops could cause such hilarity?

"Jill!" Betty Longbottom called to me from across the road. "Do you have a minute?"

I crossed over to She Sells, which from the outside appeared to be buzzing.

"It looks like business is good?"

"Very. We've never looked back since the Crustacean Monthly article."

"Is Sid here?"

"No. He's on a scuba diving course. I'll be going on it next week."

"Are you planning a scuba diving holiday?"

"No." She glanced around to make sure there was no one within earshot. "I have big news, but it's top secret at the moment. Still, I guess it will be okay to tell you. It's not like you have any friends you could blab to."

Huh?

"Sid and I have decided to start a new business venture together."

"What about She Sells?"

"That will continue as it is. In fact, the two businesses are complementary."

"Are you opening a fish and chip shop?"

"How could you suggest such a thing? I could never eat fish."

"Sorry. Just my little joke. So, what is this new business venture?"

"It's going to be called The Sea's The Limit. Catchy, eh?"

"I guess. And what will it be, exactly?"

"A marine centre. There'll be huge tanks containing all kinds of marine life. That's why Sid and I are taking the scuba diving lessons. We'll be able to swim among the fish and other sea creatures. It'll be fantastic."

"It's certainly ambitious. How will you finance it?"

"The bank is extremely pleased with our figures, and they're willing to fund most of the expansion."

"And where will it be located?"

"Right here."

I glanced up and down the street. The only shops which weren't occupied were very small. "Here, where?"

"Behind She Sells. There's a large warehouse which backs onto the shop. It's been empty for years. We're going to convert that; work should start on it next week. I'm so excited, Jill. It's everything I've ever dreamed of."

"I'm really pleased for you, Betty. I can't wait to see it."

Chapter 12

On my way back to the office, I bumped into Brent from I-Sweat, or as Deli had so succinctly put it: one of the sweaty boys.

"Hi, Brent. How's business?"

"Really good, thanks. Memberships are up this month. We haven't seen you for a while, though."

"Busy, busy. You know how it is."

"You really should keep up the exercise."

"I know. I'll try."

"We're still having that weird problem with the animal hair that appears overnight. It's a complete mystery."

"Maybe the cats from the area are working out in your gym during the night?"

He laughed. "I guess that must be it."

"I hear you've sub-let one of your rooms?"

"Yeah. It's too small for us to do anything with, so we thought we may as well make a little money from it. How did you hear?"

"Deli told me."

"She's quite a character, isn't she? Have you met her partner?"

"Nails? Oh, yeah, we go way back."

"That guy never stops biting his fingernails."

"I know, but if you ever need a decorator, he's your man."

"Good to know."

***

Jules was knitting what looked like a Christmas jumper.

"You're a bit early with that, aren't you?"

"It's for Gilbert. I figured if I started now, it might be finished in time."

"I've just seen Lules and Norman in Coffee Triangle."

"He's tutoring her on bottle tops." Jules rolled her eyes.

"Do I have any appointments this afternoon?"

"There's nothing in the diary."

"Good. Hopefully, I'll have time to get a few things sorted out."

"Paperclips or rubber bands?"

Winky was still hard at work, making his tin foil hats. He'd accumulated a large pile of them.

"How many are you planning to make?"

"As many as I can."

"How many have you sold so far?"

"None."

"Is there really any point in making more if you haven't sold a single one yet?"

"Do you want to know what your problem is?"

"I suspect you're going to tell me whether I do or not."

"You have no vision. Me? I'm what's known as a visionary."

"Okay, Mr Visionary, are you seriously trying to tell me that you expect to shift enough of these silly hats to raise the money to pay back Big Gordy?"

"Yep. Piece of cake."

You had to admire his confidence—however misplaced it might be.

I had all afternoon to review the Washbridge Flyer case. Whoops! Spoke too soon. The temperature in the room dropped dramatically. Which of my many ghost acquaintances and relatives would it be this time?

"Dad? Blodwyn? What a nice surprise."

"We haven't interrupted anything important, have we?" he said.

"Well, actually, I was just about to—"

"Good. We just had to come over, and—"

"Not so much of the 'we'," Blodwyn interjected. "I told you that Jill would be busy."

"As I was saying," he continued, regardless. "Have you heard what your mother and that Welsh clot are up to?" He started to laugh. "Guided tours of Gnome Central."

"Mum did mention it."

"Did she tell you the best bit, though? She'll be acting as the guide. I'm going to take the tour, just to see your mother squirm."

"That's not very nice, Dad."

"I don't care. Have you forgotten that she accused me of stealing her stupid gnomes? She still hasn't apologised for that."

Oh boy! Parents? Who'd have them?

My dad was still laughing about the gnome tours when Blodwyn finally managed to drag him away. At least now, I'd be able to get some work done.

Spoke too soon—again!

Luther came charging through the door.

"Sorry to burst in like this, Jill, but this is an emergency."

Jules followed him into my office; she'd obviously been powerless to stop him.

"It's okay, Jules. Make us some tea, would you?" I

waited until she was out of the room, then asked, "Whatever's wrong?"

"Someone has hacked into my computer, and they're threatening to publish all of my clients' data on the internet. If they do that, it will be the end of my business. I came to see you because I didn't know what else to do."

"Have they demanded any kind of payment?"

"No. The only thing I've received is an email that said they'd be in touch on Thursday. They said to stay by my computer, and be ready to act on their instructions. That's the day of the accountant awards."

"You'll still attend that, surely?"

"How can I with this hanging over my head? What if they release the data while I'm at the awards? I don't know what to do, Jill."

Jules brought the tea through, so I waited until she'd slopped it down on the desk.

"I might know someone who can help," I said.

"Really? How?"

"My associate is an expert with computers—particularly on the subject of hacking. If anyone can help, he can."

"That's fantastic. When can I meet him?"

"That won't be possible. My associate is what's known in the business as a 'white hat'. He's one of the good guys, but he values his anonymity above everything else. He won't agree to meet you. You'll need to give me access to your office and computer, but you can't be there when he does his thing. Can you live with that?"

"Of course, but we don't have much time."

"Leave it with me, and I'll contact my associate as soon as I can. Once I've got hold of him, I'll let you know when we need access to your office. Okay?"

"Yeah. Thanks, Jill. My whole career is in your hands."

No pressure, then.

As Luther was leaving, he glanced over at the corner of the room.

"Are those tin foil hats?"

"Err—yeah. Jack is having a conspiracy theory themed party at his office. I said I'd help out by making the tin foil hats."

"Oh? Cool."

As soon as he was out of the office, I called Winky out from under the sofa.

"You'll have to find somewhere to store those hats. People will think I'm some kind of nutter if they see them."

"That boat has long since sailed."

"I need a favour."

"I figured as much when I heard you talking about *white hats*. Like you know what that means." He scoffed.

"I need you to get hold of Tibby the Hack."

"He's on holiday."

"For how long?"

"He's on the Norfolk Broads for a couple of weeks."

"Can you get him back here?"

"Not a chance. Tibby loves his boating. I do know someone else who could help, though."

"Who?"

"Tubby the Hack."

"Tubby?"

"He's Tibby's fatter, older cousin."

"Is he any good?"

"He taught Tibby everything he knows."

"Great. Can you get him to come and see me PDQ?"

"Tubby doesn't come cheap."

"Surely, you can get him to do me a good deal?"

"It seems like ages since I had any red salmon."

"Okay. I'll buy some."

"How much?"

"Lots. Now, will you get hold of Tubby?"

At least that was sorted. Now, I could get back to the Washbridge Flyer case.

"Sorry to trouble you, Jill." Jules popped her head around the door.

"What is it?"

"There's a young woman here who would like to see you. Shall I tell her you're too busy?"

"Who is it?"

"She said her name is Alicia."

Great! That was all I needed.

"Show her in."

"Shall I make more drinks?"

"No. Don't bother. She might poison it."

"Sorry?"

"Never mind. Just show her in."

"Thanks for seeing me, Jill." Alicia edged towards my desk, but didn't sit down.

"What do you want? I'm very busy."

"I'll only take up a few minutes of your time."

"I'm listening."

"I know you don't trust me."

"I wonder why?"

"I don't blame you, but I really am trying to make a new

start with Glen."

"So you said. Just don't expect me to believe it."

"That's why I came here today. I was hoping that there was something I could do to convince you that I mean what I say."

"I highly doubt it."

"Ma Chivers still wants you and your grandmother gone, you know. What if I could find information that you could use against her?"

"And how do you propose to do that? From what I hear, Ma Chivers has washed her hands of you."

"I still know lots of people who are close to her. Some of them are as disillusioned as I became, but are too afraid to make the break from her."

"Why do we need your help? We seem to be doing just fine by ourselves."

"That's just it. She'll wait until your guard is down, and then she'll strike. I may be able to warn you when that's going to happen. What do you have to lose by agreeing?"

"Do what you like. As I've said before, I'll judge you on your actions not on your words because we've already established they're worthless."

"Okay. Thanks for hearing me out, Jill."

And with that, she skulked out of my office.

***

I gave up trying to work on the Washbridge Flyer case, and decided to call it a day. On my way out, I found Lules with her sister, in the outer office.

"Hi, Lules. How's the swotting going?"

"Brilliantly. Norman is a great teacher. I'm going to

knock them dead at the Miss Bottle Top competition."

"That's fantastic."

"Ask me a question, Jill."

"Sorry?"

"About bottle tops. Go on, ask me anything."

"Okay. Who in their right mind would want to collect them?"

Jules laughed. Lules didn't.

"I'm sorry," I said. "When is the competition?"

"Tomorrow night."

"I'm sure you'll do just great. Anyway, I'm going to call it a day. Bye, both of you."

When I got to the toll bridge, Mr Ivers was still wearing the sling; he looked very fed up.

"How are the elbows, Mr Ivers?"

"Still giving me grief."

"No luck replacing Bert, then?"

"Not even a sniff."

It was then that I had one of my brilliant ideas.

What? Of course I have them. Haven't you noticed? Sheesh!

"I might just know someone who will do the job, Mr Ivers."

"Really?" His face lit up. "Who?"

"A friend of mine. He's fallen on hard times recently. I can have a word with him if you like?"

"Yes please, Jill."

Fortunately, Jack wasn't home, so I was able to magic myself over to the bridge on the road to North Candle.

"Give me some money!" Cole appeared from

underneath the bridge.

"It's only me."

"Oh, hello, Jill."

"I may have some good news for you."

"I could really do with some."

"How would you feel about working in the human world?"

"Doing what?"

"It just so happens I may have found the ideal job for you. It's based on a bridge, and all you have to do is collect money from the people who cross it."

"I can do that. It's what I specialise in."

"I know. That's just what I thought."

"But I'm worried about being in the human world. Won't I stand out?"

"Not at all. The human you'll be working with is so weird that no one will notice you. What do you say?"

"How would I get there?"

"If you're interested, I could magic you over there now?"

"I'm scared."

"You were afraid to go to Candlefield, but it was okay, wasn't it?"

"Yeah. I enjoyed it, actually."

"There you go, then. And besides, you need the money."

"I really do." He took a deep breath. "Okay, let's do it."

I grabbed his hand before he could change his mind, and magicked us over to the toll bridge.

"Mr Ivers!"

"Jill? Where did you come from?"

"This is Cole who I told you about. He's had lots of experience collecting cash on bridges."

"That's fantastic." Mr Ivers opened the door to the pay booth. "Come in, Cole. You can start straightaway."

I gave Cole the thumbs up, and then hurried back home.

Another satisfied customer.

Chapter 13

The next morning, after I'd showered and dressed, I found Jack staring out of the lounge window.

"What are you looking at, nosey?"

"I'm not nosey. I'm just taking a healthy interest in our neighbours."

"Why is it that when I take a healthy interest in something, I'm being nosey, but when you do it, that's okay?"

"Those new neighbours across the road are seriously weird."

"They're rude—that's for sure."

"They have all the curtains closed."

"Maybe they just prefer the dark."

"They're probably vampires." He grinned.

"That must be it. Maybe Blossom is a witch, too?"

"Now you're being silly. Blossom is an old dear. We should ask her over for dinner sometime. She must be lonely in that big house all by herself."

"Maybe, but not this week. Will you be home for dinner tonight?"

"I'll be late because I have to sort out my dress suit."

"Make sure you get a receipt so we can claim the money back from Grandma."

"Did she say she'd pay?"

"I did."

After Jack had left for work, and before I left for the office, I called Desmond Sidings.

"It's Jill Gooder. Sorry to call at this hour."

"Not a problem. I'm an early riser."

"I'd like to take a look around The Flyer. How soon could you arrange that?"

"It's not possible at the moment because the police still have it locked down as a crime scene."

"Okay. Will you let me know when they release it?"

"Will do."

"In the meantime, I'd like to check a few things with you. How many members of staff are typically on board the trips?"

"Typically, just two: the driver, and the guard who is also responsible for the buffet."

"Just those two? Really?"

"Yes. We have to keep costs to a minimum."

"How can the guard do everything by himself?"

"The drinks and snacks that are available are all pretty basic: Sandwiches, crisps, that sort of thing."

"Am I right in thinking that there's no way for the engine driver to access the carriages while the train is moving?"

"Correct. The only way to do that is to get out of the engine, and walk down the platform."

"How many stops does The Flyer make?"

"It doesn't. It effectively travels in a large circle. Most of the passengers are only there for the experience of travelling on a steam train."

"Okay. Just one last question. It appears that there were different guards on the two journeys. Is that usual?"

"Thomas West handed in his notice after the first trip. That's why Stephen Pearce was on the second trip."

"Okay, Desmond, that's very helpful. Don't forget to let me know when I can see the train."

It occurred to me that Stanley Sidcup and Barbara Hawthorne might have been on The Flyer when Carol Strand was murdered, so I gave them both a call.

"Hello?" Stanley sounded distracted.

"Stanley, it's Jill Gooder."

"Is it urgent, Jill? Only the parrot has just got out of its cage. Momsy was trying to clean it out, and it flew off."

"I just wondered if you were on The Flyer on Sunday?"

"No. I decided to give it a miss. Momsy and I went to see her sister instead. Glad I did as it turned out. Terrible business. Sorry, I must go. I need to catch this silly bird."

"Okay. Thanks, Stanley. Good luck with the parrot."

"Is that Barbara? It's Jill Gooder."

"Hello, there. I imagine you're calling about this awful murder?"

"That's right. Were you on The Flyer on Sunday?"

"I was. I couldn't believe it."

"Did you see anything?"

"Nothing at all, but then I was busy trying to dry off my dress."

"Sorry?"

"The stupid guard knocked a glass of wine out of my hand—all over my dress. I wouldn't have minded, but I only bought it last Friday."

"Was the woman who was murdered in your carriage?"

"I believe so, according to what I heard, but I can honestly say I didn't even notice her. Apparently, she was seated at the opposite end, near to the toilet. Sorry I can't be of more help."

"That's okay. Thanks anyway."

Cole took my cash at the toll bridge. He looked much happier than when he'd been on the deserted bridge in Candlefield. As I was about to drive off, Mr Ivers came out of the booth, and flagged me down.

"Where did you find this guy, Jill?"

"Why? Is there a problem?"

"Quite the opposite. The man is a marvel. It's like he's been doing the job all his life."

"I did tell you that he'd had experience in this type of work."

"My elbows can't thank you enough. He is rather quiet, though. I've tried to engage him in conversation a few times, but without much success."

"He's probably still nervous. I'm sure he'll come out of his shell in time."

"That's probably it. Maybe I should offer to show him my collection of bottle tops. That's always a good ice breaker."

"Why not? Go for it."

Poor Cole. Snigger.

***

Mrs V looked resplendent in her green ballgown. There were two other gowns hanging from the coat stand.

"What do you think, Jill?" She did a little twirl.

"It's very nice. I assume it's for the competition on Saturday?"

"That's right. One's dress shouldn't really be taken into consideration; it should be all about the dancing. But I've been around the block enough times to realise that it really does matter. Which one do you prefer?"

"I'd need to see you wearing them, but the green one is very nice."

"Chartreuse."

"Sorry?"

"This gown is chartreuse."

"Okay. The pink and blue ones look nice too."

"You mean cerise and ultramarine?"

"Whatever."

"I'll slip the others on, and come through to your office, so you can tell me which one you like best."

"Okay."

The pile of tin foil hats in the corner of the room was halfway up the wall.

"How many more of those stupid silver hats do you intend to make?"

"Excuse me, but they aren't *silver* hats; they're *argent*."

"Don't you start. I don't suppose you've actually sold any yet?"

"No, but I expect the rush to start any day now."

The poor cat was delusional. "If I were you, I'd forget the silly hats, pack my bags, and get out of Dodge, before Big Gordy comes a-looking."

"You worry way too much. I have everything in hand."

"I hope so. I've just had this room decorated—I don't want it spraying with your blood."

Just before ten o'clock, Mr Gander turned up, unexpectedly. Mrs V, who had changed into the pink— whoops, I mean *cerise* gown, showed him through to my office.

"Why is your receptionist wearing a ballgown?" He had the same confused look that so many visitors to my office seemed to share.

"She has an important ballroom dancing competition coming up."

"I see." He clearly didn't. "I assume you heard about the murder on The Flyer at the weekend?"

"I did."

"That proves conclusively that Gary didn't murder Gena. He must have been a victim too."

"It certainly looks that way." I saw no reason to mention Don Preston—it would serve no purpose now.

"In view of this, we will no longer require your services. Would you send your bill for the time you've spent on this to-date?"

"Of course."

When it was time to show Mr Gander out, Mrs V was wearing the ultramarine gown.

"So?" she said, after he'd left. "Which one do you prefer?"

"They're all nice, but I particularly like the err—green—err—chartr—err—the first one."

"Me too. Chartreuse it is then."

***

Sonya Aynos, whose husband had gone missing, had arranged for me to meet with his best friends, Roy Wright and Philip Long, in Spooky Wooky.

Behind the counter, Harry was wearing a shirt adorned with a pleasing pattern consisting of thousands of tiny letter 'H's. Larry was wearing a similar one, but with the letter 'L'.

"Nice shirts, guys."

"Thanks, Jill." Harry smiled. "We got them from Alphabet Wear. They have some fabulous stuff in their shop. Have you seen it?"

"I can't say I have, but I've barely explored any of GT yet."

"I saw a lovely 'J' dress that would really suit you," Larry said.

"I'll have to check it out sometime. Where is it exactly?"

"Do you know the statues in the market place?"

"You mean the creepy vegetables-with-legs statues?"

Both Harry and Larry looked horrified.

"They aren't creepy!" Harry sounded indignant. "They're fabulous."

"I didn't mean *creepy* in the bad sense of the word. Gosh, no. I think they're—err—quite magnificent. I meant that they look as though they can creep around—seeing as how they have legs. That's all."

"Hmm?" Harry looked unconvinced, but continued, "Alphabet Wear is on Spirit Lane which is just behind the statues."

"Great. I'll check it out later. In the meantime, I'll have my usual, please."

"I should have mentioned earlier. Those two men in the corner said they were supposed to meet you here."

"Right, thanks."

Once I had my coffee and muffin, I made my way over to the corner table.

"Excuse me. I'm Jill Gooder.

"Phillip Long." The taller of the two men stood up.

"And you must be Roy Wright?"

"Actually, Roy couldn't make it," Philip said. "He's laid up with flu. This is my brother, Paul. He knows Malcolm Aynos too."

That was all well and good, but two Longs didn't make a Wright.

What? Come on! You know you love it.

"How was Malcolm the last time you saw him?"

"He was really down," Philip said. "I've never seen him like that. He loved his job at the gnome factory, and was devastated when they let him go. He'd been in that same job for years, and had no idea how to go about getting another one. Malcolm doesn't even have a computer. That's why I suggested he could use mine to see if he could find any suitable vacancies. In fact, that was the last time I saw him. I set him up on my computer, and went out for a few hours. When I came back, he'd gone."

"Do you think I could take a look at your computer? Maybe the browser history will give me some clues as to which websites he'd been looking at."

"Sure. We can go back to my place now, if you like?"

So that's what we did. Philip Long logged me onto his computer, and I checked the browser history.

"What's Hot Ghosts?" I asked.

"Oh, err—nothing. You can ignore that."

"Are you sure? There seem to be a lot of entries for that particular website."

"Those have nothing to do with Malcolm." By now, Philip was looking decidedly uncomfortable. Only then, did the penny drop, and I realised why he didn't want me to pursue that particular line of enquiry. "What about this? Ghostlancers? What's that?"

"I've no idea." Philip shrugged.

When I clicked on the link, it took me to a website that recruited ghosts to work on freelance projects both in GT and in the human world. The website obviously used cookies because it offered to display recently viewed projects. As soon as I clicked on that link, everything started to fall into place.

"Do you have a recent photo of Malcolm that I could see?"

"Yeah." Philip took out his phone. "That was taken last year."

Eureka!

Chapter 14

After leaving Spooky Wooky, I called Murray to tell him that I wanted to hide in the writing room again the following day. He wasn't sure that would achieve anything, but I was now confident it would pay dividends—although not necessarily for Murray.

I was intrigued to see the shop where Harry and Larry had bought their shirts, even if that did mean I'd have to walk past those hideous and very creepy statues. As always, there were lots of people taking selfies in front of the monstrous legged vegetables. I was rapidly coming to the conclusion that ghosts had a particularly weird taste when it came to statues.

Alphabet Wear was a tiny shop, sandwiched in-between two (ironically enough) sandwich shops.

"Hi," a bubbly young woman, with custard coloured hair, greeted me as soon as I stepped inside. "I'm Dee."

"Hi. I'm Jill."

"Is this your first visit to Alphabet Wear?"

"It is. Two friends told me about your shop."

"Hi." A second assistant, just as bubbly, swooped in from somewhere. "I'm Bea. Do you need any help, or do you understand how things work?"

"I'm okay, thanks." *How things work?* How difficult could it be to choose a dress, try it on, and then pay for it?

Dee and Bea left me to browse, but I could sense them keeping an eye on me.

The shop stocked an extensive range of clothing for both men and women of all ages. Every item had a pattern made up of a single letter. I really wanted a dress, but none of the 'J's caught my eye. Then I spotted a lovely summer dress with a 'G' pattern. I took it off the rail, and was on my way to the changing room when Dee intercepted me.

"Excuse me, did you say your name was Jill?"

"That's right."

"Is that Jill with a 'J', or Gill with a 'G'?"

"Jill with a 'J'."

"In that case, you can't buy that dress."

"Why not?"

"It's a 'G'."

"Yeah. It's beautiful."

"But it's a 'G'."

"So?"

"You're only allowed to buy items with a letter 'J' design."

I laughed, but she didn't. "Are you serious?"

"Totally. I'm sorry."

"My surname is Gooder. G for Gooder."

"I'm afraid that doesn't count. It's the initial letter of your first name which matters."

"I really love this dress. Is there no way you could make an exception?"

"I don't think so, but I could ask the manager, if you like?"

"Please."

She disappeared into the back, and returned a few minutes later, accompanied by an older woman.

"Hello. My name is Gigi. Dee has explained the situation, but I'm afraid there's nothing to be done. You're only allowed to purchase 'J' patterned garments."

I left the shop empty-handed, but I wasn't going to

allow their stupid rules to stop me from buying that dress.

I cast a spell to make myself look like Kathy. I know—I wasn't thrilled about it, but needs must.

"Hi, I'm Dee. Is this your first visit to Alphabet Wear?"

"It is. My name is Gloria. Can I see dresses with a 'G' pattern, please?"

***

Back in Washbridge, I dropped my dress off at the car, and then made my way to the office. En route, who should I bump into but Peter; he looked as white as a sheet.

"Peter? Are you okay?"

"Not really."

"What's wrong? It's not Kathy or the kids, is it?"

"No, everyone's fine. Do you remember I told you about the new contract that I'd just won?"

"At Washbridge Country Hall?"

"Yeah. Look, I know you're going to think I'm crazy, but the rumours about that place are right."

"What rumours?"

"Don't you remember? I told you the previous contractors had walked away because they'd claimed the maze was haunted."

"Are you trying to tell me that—?"

"It really is haunted. Yeah. I saw them with my own eyes."

"Ghosts?"

"Yeah. They were as real as you are. One of them had his head under his arm!"

"Come on." I laughed.

"It's true, honestly. I had to leave without finishing trimming the hedges. I'll have to tell the owners that I can't continue with the contract."

"Kathy won't be thrilled. She's got her heart set on a new car."

"I know, but what can I do? I'm still shaking." He held out his hands.

"Why don't you take a break, and then try again? It's possible that all the stories you've heard about the place have made your imagination work overtime."

"But the ghosts were so real."

"It's surprising what the mind can do. You could give it a few hours, and then go back. If the ghosts are still there, you can still quit."

"You're right. I can't just walk away without at least making sure it wasn't all in my mind. Thanks, Jill. I'm sorry for acting so crazy. You won't say anything to Kathy, will you?"

"Of course not."

***

Tubby the Hack's name was well deserved. *Tubby*, I mean. As for '*the Hack*', we'd see about that. The overweight cat and Winky were both sitting on my desk. It was just as well that the desk was a solid antique—a flatpack model would have collapsed under their combined weight.

Winky made the introductions, "Jill, this is Tubby. Tubby, meet Jill Gooder."

"How much does this job pay?" Tubby got straight down to business.

"What's your usual rate?"

"More than you can afford, by the look of this place. I'm only here as a favour to Winky."

"I'm very grateful. How about we say that you'll get half of whatever Winky makes on his tin foil hats?"

"That sounds fair." Tubby nodded his approval.

"Hold on!" Winky objected. "You can't use my profits to pay Tubby."

"Yes, I can because I've allowed you to use my office to manufacture and store the hats. Unless, of course, you'd rather I dumped them out of the window."

"No! Okay. Tubby can have half the profits."

"Do we have a deal, Tubby?"

"Sure. What do you need me to do?"

"It's my accountant who is having the problem. We'll need to go over to his office."

"Okay. Let's do it."

I fetched Winky's cat basket out of the cupboard. "You'll need to get in here."

"Into that thing? No chance."

"You have to. They're never going to let you into his office building otherwise."

"You never mentioned any of this?" He glared at Winky.

"Sorry, bro. You'll be okay. How about if you have some salmon first?"

"Okay. I suppose so."

"You heard the man, Jill. Break out the salmon."

"Okay."

"Red, not pink."

"Naturally."

"For two."

Tubby moaned and groaned all the way over to Luther's office. He was a cat who obviously did not appreciate being kept in a basket. I'd called ahead to tell Luther that he would need to vacate his office while I and my 'associate' checked what had happened to his computer.

Once inside the office, I opened the basket, and let Tubby out.

"If I'd known how long I'd have to be in that thing, I'd have requested double the fee." He stretched.

"Too late. A deal's a deal." I walked over to the desk. "Oh no! Luther hasn't logged in, and I have no idea what his password is."

"Not a problem." Tubby ran his paws over the keyboard, and moments later he was in.

"How did you do that?"

"Trade secret. Now, let's see what's going on here."

"Can I help?"

"I don't think so." He grinned. "Why don't you take a seat over there, and file your nails or something?"

"File my—?" I bit my tongue before I said something I'd regret. I'd just have to save my indignation until after he'd finished the job.

"What?" He laughed at something on screen. "You have to be kidding. Pathetic."

Something obviously had him amused, but I couldn't work out if that was good or bad.

"Amateurs!" he pronounced, and then turned to me.

"Do you know what's going on?" I asked.

"In a word: nothing."

"What do you mean?"

"I mean that there is nothing going on with this computer. The warning message about publishing the client data is bunkum. Whoever did this, has no meaningful access to the computer. The only thing they've managed to do is send that stupid warning message."

"Are you sure about that?"

He gave me a disparaging look.

"Okay, sorry. Of course you are. Is there any way you can trace who sent the message?"

"Sure. Piece of cake. Just give me a minute."

In fact, it took him less than that. When I saw who was behind the empty threat, everything suddenly made sense.

"That's great, Tubby."

"No problem."

"There's just one more thing I need you to do."

I explained what I had in mind, and he got straight onto it.

Now, I was going to have some fun.

***

The offices of accountant, Seymour Sums, were in a building only two doors down from Luther's office. I offered to run Tubby home first, but he said he'd rather make his own way than have to get back in the cat basket.

"Can I help you?" The po-faced receptionist glared at the cat basket. "You can't bring an animal in here."

"It's okay. This is empty." I opened the flap to prove the

point.

"What do you want?"

"I'd like to see Mr Sums."

"Do you have an appointment?"

"No."

"In that case, I'm—"

She stopped dead, mid-sentence, as the 'sleep' spell kicked in. I really couldn't be bothered to waste time, arguing with her.

"Who are you? How did you get in here?" Seymour Sums looked at me over the half-moon glasses that were propped on the very end of his nose.

"It doesn't matter who I am."

"This is outrageous!" He flushed red with anger. "Daphne! Call security!"

"Daphne is taking a snooze. Now, why don't you and I have a talk about cybercrime?"

"What are you talking about? I'd like you to leave right now!"

"What was the plan, Seymour? To get Luther Stone to withdraw from the awards?"

Shocked, he sat down. "I don't know what you're—"

"Don't bother to deny it. I know you sent that message, threatening to publish his clients' data. I also know that you aren't capable of doing any such thing because you, dear sir, are a rank amateur. What do you have to say now?"

"No comment."

"Maybe I can help to jog your memory." I walked around his desk. "May I?" I didn't wait for him to respond. Instead, I typed in the command that Tubby had given to me.

"What's that?" He pointed to the on-screen message.

"I would have thought it was self-explanatory. All of your files will be permanently deleted in two minutes from now. One minute, fifty-nine, fifty-eight."

He reached out towards the power switch.

"I wouldn't do that. If you switch the computer off, the files will be erased immediately."

"This is a bluff."

"Actually, it isn't. I have an associate who knows how to access and take control of any computer. If you think it's a bluff, why not let the clock run down? That should prove it one way or another."

He glanced at the timer which was now down to one minute and thirty-two seconds.

"What do you want?"

"The truth, for starters."

"Okay. I sent the message to Stone. I've lost out on the award for the last two years. I couldn't bear to lose out again. Stone is the only one standing in my way."

"You're a real piece of work, do you know that?"

"I'm sorry. Please stop the timer. If my files are erased, I'll have no business left."

"Surely you keep back-ups?"

"I—err—I haven't done any for a while."

"When was the last time you did them?"

"I don't remember."

"Oh dear."

"Please! Stop the timer!"

I typed in a second command. The timer stopped, and then disappeared from the screen.

"Thank you. What happens now?"

"That will be up to Luther."

Chapter 15

Once I was in the car, I called Luther and told him that Seymour Sums had been responsible for the threat.

"What about my client data, Jill? How can I be sure it won't be published?"

"It's perfectly safe. In fact, there was never any danger that it would be published. The message you saw was no more than a hoax."

"Are you sure about that?"

"Absolutely. My associate checked it out thoroughly. You can stop worrying."

"That's such a relief. Seymour and I have never been what you'd call close, but I still can't believe that he'd stoop so low as to do something like this."

"He was obviously desperate to get you out of the picture so that he'd be in with a chance of winning the award. What would you like to do about him? The police take a dim view of this kind of cybercrime. Would you like me to pass on the information I have to them?"

"No, don't do that. I have no desire to destroy the man."

"How about I tell Sums that he has to drop out of the awards competition? That sounds fair."

"No. If I win the award, I want to win it on merit, and not by default. From what you've told me, it sounds like you put the fear of god into Seymour. That will be punishment enough."

"You're a very generous man, Luther. I'm not sure I'd be so compassionate if I were in your shoes."

"Thanks again for your help, Jill. I don't know what I would have done without it. And, please thank your associate, too. Are you sure he doesn't want any payment?"

"Not unless you have any red salmon going spare."

"Sorry?"

"Nothing. Just my little joke. Good luck with the awards, Luther."

***

I'd told Peter that I didn't think he had anything to worry about with regard to the haunted maze, but if he and the previous contractors had all seen ghosts, there had to be something going on. If the ghosts were still there when he went back, Peter would no doubt quit the job too. That wouldn't go down well with Kathy who had her heart set on a new car. I wanted to check the maze for myself, to find out what was going on. First, though, I magicked myself over to GT, to get some advice from Constance Bowler.

"Hi, Jill. This is a pleasant surprise."

"Sorry for dropping in unannounced."

"No problem. What can I do for you?"

"I'd like to pick your brains."

"Sure."

"My brother-in-law, Peter, has a landscaping business in the human world. He's recently taken on a contract at a country house; part of the work involves the maintenance of a maze. Before he started on the job, he told me that the previous contractors had quit because they claimed the maze was haunted. And now, Peter also reckons that he's seen ghosts in the maze."

"Have you checked it out yourself?"

"Not yet, but I intend to. What I don't understand is

how the ghosts are making themselves visible to whoever happens to venture into the maze. Don't they have to attach themselves before they can be seen?"

"It's quite complicated. Generally speaking, you're right, but there is a potion based on the spookberry plant, which will allow a ghost to be visible to all and sundry. That's what's used by the companies who employ ghosts to work in the human world. The people running the ghost train scam must have used a variation of it."

"I assume Hauntings Unlimited must use it too?"

"Yes, but the potion's use is strictly controlled. It's only available under a licence issued by the GT authorities."

"Do you think the ghosts in the maze might be using the potion?"

"It sounds like it, but I'd be surprised if they have a licence for its use. Chances are, they'll have purchased it on the black market."

"Thanks, Constance. That's very helpful."

"Do you need me to provide any support?"

"I don't think that will be necessary. I've got this one."

***

There was a large noticeboard at the entrance to Washbridge Country Hall. On it was a plan of the grounds, which showed the maze was to the rear of the property. The hall was only open to visitors at the weekends. If I'd tried to walk through the grounds, I would no doubt have been stopped by the staff, so rather than have to face a lot of awkward questions, I made myself invisible. Once inside the maze, I reversed the 'invisible' spell, and tried to find my way to the centre.

Emphasis on 'tried'.

Mazes have to be the stupidest thing in the world. I mean, what's the point?

What? No, I'm not just saying that because I got lost a dozen times.

I was getting more and more frustrated when suddenly two ghostly figures appeared in front of me. They were both dressed in Victorian clothing; one of them was carrying his head under his arm.

"Whoooo!" The one with his head still on his shoulders wailed.

"Do me a favour!" I was in no mood for this nonsense.

"Whoooo!" He tried again.

"You two are pathetic. And you." I pointed to the headless one. "Put your head back on your shoulders. You aren't impressing anyone."

He did as he was told, and then said, "Who are you? Why aren't you scared?"

"Scared of you two comedians? I don't think so."

"She's a sup," the other ghost said.

"And you two are in big trouble."

"We haven't done anything wrong."

"You've been scaring humans."

"We were only having a bit of fun. You should see their faces when I take my head off."

"It's no laughing matter. What are your names?"

"I'm Bobby Blue," the ghost with the detachable head said.

"And I'm Billy Blue."

"You're the Blues brothers?"

"Yeah. We've lived in the maze for over a hundred years."

"And you've been scaring people all that time?"

"No. We'd never shown ourselves to anyone until a few months ago. We weren't able to until then."

"That's when you started to use the spookberry potion?"

"Yeah. It's great. Life's a lot more interesting now."

"You do realise that it's illegal to use that potion without a licence, don't you?"

They exchanged a glance, and then both shook their heads.

"Well it is. If I report you, you'll be in big trouble with the GT authorities."

"Don't do that, please. We like it here in the maze."

"I'll need you to give me what's left of the spookberry potion."

"Okay," Bobby said. "I'll go and get it for you."

"Where did you get the potion from?" I asked Billy while his brother went to fetch it.

"A travelling salesman."

"Name?"

"Will he get in trouble?"

"Probably, but if you don't tell me, you definitely will."

"Okay. His name was Homer Range. You won't tell him that I gave you his name, will you?"

"Don't worry. I won't mention you."

Bobby returned and passed me the bottle, which was still half full. After pouring the contents away, I gave the two ghosts another stern warning, then made myself invisible and left.

***

I was on my way home; I'd decided to call it a day. Cole was taking cash in the toll booth.

"Hi, Jill."

"How's it going, Cole? Still enjoying the work?"

"It's brilliant. I used to get really bored, waiting for people to cross my old bridge, but here, there are people crossing all the time."

"He's doing really well." Mr Ivers appeared behind Cole. "He's a natural."

"That's very nice of you to say, Monty. You're an excellent teacher," Cole said, and then turned to me. "Are you interested in bottle tops, Jill?"

"Not really, no."

"I wasn't either. Not until Monty shared his knowledge with me. They really are fascinating."

"That's great, but I'd better get going. I have dinner to make."

When I parked on the drive, Megan was on the front, mowing her lawn.

"Hi, Jill. I thought I'd better give the lawn a cut. It doesn't look very good if a professional gardener can't look after her own garden."

"Ours could do with cutting too. I'll get Jack on it."

"Have you seen the new neighbours?" She gestured across the road.

"We had a cup of tea with Blossom. She seems really nice, but I doubt she'll be here long. She's moved up here to be near her daughter, and she's only renting that place until she can find something more suitable."

"What about those other two?" Megan pulled a face. "Couple of weirdos, if you ask me."

"They did seem rather odd when we went around to introduce ourselves."

"They never open the curtains, but I've seen them, peering out every now and then. They've always got balaclavas on. That's pretty weird if you ask me."

"At least they don't play the bagpipes. How are things with Ryan?"

"Don't ask."

I wished I hadn't. When would I ever learn? "What's wrong now?"

"It's probably just me being silly, but last weekend, he said he was going to visit his mum and dad. When I said I'd like to go with him, he started acting strange."

"How do you mean: strange?"

"If he'd said that he thought it was a bit early in our relationship for me to meet his parents, I would have understood, but he was just really weird. When I asked where they lived, he got all flustered, and then made some stupid excuse and said he had to leave."

"I'm sure it doesn't mean anything."

"I think he's ashamed to let his parents know that I used to be a model. A lot of people can be funny about that kind of thing. They hear stories and get all kinds of weird ideas in their heads."

"I'm sure you're over-reacting."

"Do you really think so?"

"I'm positive. Maybe he just had a lot on his mind. The betting shop must be quite stressful."

"I suppose you're right. Maybe I'm just being oversensitive."

What was it with Ryan? When was he ever going to get a clue? It looked like yet another visit to WashBets was called for.

I was just about to go into the house when Megan called me back.

"Sorry, Jill, I was so wrapped up in my silly problems that I totally forgot to mention your sandpit."

"What about it?"

"It's probably nothing, but when I was looking out of my upstairs window, I noticed that there seemed to be lots of footprints in the sand."

"Do you think someone has been around the back of the house?"

"I don't think it was a person. They look like animal footprints."

"It's probably a cat."

"Yeah, I guess so, but I thought I should mention it."

"Thanks, Megan. I'll take a look."

The footprints most definitely did not belong to a cat. In fact, they weren't like any animal footprints I'd ever seen; they were perfectly square in shape.

I smelled a rat. A grandma-shaped rat. She'd tricked me into believing that sand demons were a thing, when in fact they didn't even exist. Maybe she wasn't aware that Aunt Lucy had put me right on that score. This was probably the second phase of her silly ruse. If it was, then it was a pretty poor effort—it would have been obvious to anyone that these weren't real animal foot—

"Hello." A tiny creature popped its head up through the sand. "I'm Joey." He climbed out of the sandpit, and shook some of the sand from his long fur.

"What are you?"

"I'm a sand sloth."

The small creature had long, unkempt fur, which was still matted with sand. On the end of his short stubby legs were square-shaped paws.

"What are you doing here?"

"I have nowhere else to go. I used to live with my brother, Wally, but he's got himself a girlfriend now, and he's kicked me out. I spent all day looking for another sandpit until I found yours. Can I stay here, please?"

"I—err—can't you go to the seaside? There's a lot of sand there."

"The salt from the sea is poisonous to us. That's why we live in sandpits. I won't be any trouble, I promise. You won't even know I'm here."

"My neighbour has already seen your footprints."

"Sorry. I promise I'll cover them up in future."

"What about when my niece and her friends come over?"

"If you let me know when they're coming, I'll make myself scarce until they've gone."

"What about—err—I mean—will there be any mess?"

"Oh goodness, no. Sand sloths don't need to—we don't have to—you know."

"How can that possibly be? No, wait, don't tell me. I don't need to know."

"So? Can I stay? I don't know where I'll go if you turn me away."

"Okay. We'll see how it goes, but if you cause any problems, you'll have to leave."

"Thank you so much." He jumped back into the sandpit, and disappeared under the sand.

When I walked into the house, I heard noises coming

from the kitchen.

"Hello?"

"Hi." Jack poked his head around the door.

"I didn't hear your car. I thought we had burglars."

"No. Only me. I've just come in."

"I was around the back. I was — err — "

"Talking to the sandpit? Yes, I saw you. What is it with you and that sandpit? You've been acting weird ever since we had it installed."

"Don't be silly. I was just — err — talking to the plants. It helps with their growth."

Chapter 16

The next morning, before I set off for work, I did a quick check of the sandpit. There were no footprints—square or otherwise—to be seen. Joey seemed to be as good as his word.

Jules and Lules were in the office. Lules looked particularly pleased with herself.

"I won, Jill. I won Miss Bottle Top!"

"That's great. Well done, you."

"I couldn't have done it without Norman's help. I answered every question correctly. The other contestants knew next to nothing about bottle tops."

"How did you get on with Norman?"

"Really well. He's great fun. It's a pity he already has a girlfriend."

Unbelievable. Whatever it was that Norman had (and it certainly wasn't brains), he should bottle it and sell it.

"That's not all, Jill." Lules was bursting to tell me the rest of her news. "I've been offered two modelling assignments already: one for a company that makes fizzy drinks, and the other for a bottle manufacturing company."

"That's fantastic."

"I have to hold my hands up, and say I was wrong," Jules admitted. "The competition has obviously been a good thing for Lules' career."

"Thanks, sis."

"Is Mrs V coming in today?" I asked.

"No. She said that she and Armi were going to spend the whole day practising for the ballroom dancing competition."

Inside my office, there was a queue of cats, all waiting to be served by Winky.

"Patience, everyone," he said, from his position on the sofa. "There's enough to go around."

"I'll take three," the Persian at the front of the queue held out a twenty-pound note.

"Sorry." Winky shook his head. "You know the rules. Two per person maximum." He handed two of the tin foil hats to the disgruntled Persian.

I had lots of paperwork to catch up on, but I was way too intrigued to focus. Instead, I spent the next hour watching Winky selling his silly little hats. By the time everyone had been served, the pile of hats was half its former size.

"I don't get it," I said, once he and I were alone in the office.

"Don't get what?" He didn't look up—he was too busy counting his takings.

"Why the sudden demand for tin foil hats?"

He shrugged.

"And how could you possibly know this would happen?" I pressed him.

"Let's just say I can read the trends."

"You still have quite a few left."

"These will be gone by tomorrow. In fact, I plan on making more tonight."

There was more to this than met the eye; he was up to something, but I had no idea what it was.

***

I was determined to track down Helen Drewmore's descendants. Finding them was the only chance I had of discovering more about what I'd seen and heard at CASS.

Just as Aunt Lucy had said, the Candlefield Electoral Society was located in Candlefield town hall. The young vampire who worked there was extremely helpful; she checked their records, and provided me with a list of the people in Candlefield who had the surname: Drewmore; there were only four of them.

The first two: Karen and Brian Drewmore lived at the same address—presumably man and wife? I found their phone number from the Candlefield phone directory, but there was no answer when I called, and no answerphone on which to leave a message. I'd have to try them again later.

Charles Drewmore answered on the first ring. He was a little cautious at first, but when I explained what I was trying to do, he couldn't have been more helpful. It turned out that he had a keen interest in tracing his own family tree, and had done lots of research over recent years. That sounded promising until he told me that his research had not uncovered anyone named Helen Drewmore. He was quite sure that the person I was looking for, although they shared the same surname, was not a relative of his.

I called the last person on my list.

"Hello?"

"Is that Cynthia Drewmore?"

"Who's that?"

"My name is Jill Gooder. I was hoping to speak with Cynthia Drewmore."

"I'm Cynthia."

"Right. This is going to sound kind of weird, but I'm trying to trace someone who lived a long time ago. Her name was Helen Drewmore." I waited for a reaction, but there was none, so I continued, "Do you happen to know if any of your ancestors were called Helen?"

"What's this all about?"

"It's rather a long and complicated story, I'm afraid."

"I'm rather busy at the moment. You've caught me in the middle of baking."

"I'm sorry. If you could just tell me if you're aware of anyone called Helen Drewmore, then I'll be out of your hair."

"Come and see me tomorrow."

"Err — right. Does that mean you do know her?"

"We can discuss it tomorrow, at midday. Do you have my address?"

"Yes."

"I'll see you tomorrow, then."

Before I could ask any more questions, she'd hung up. I had no idea what to make of that. Why did she want to meet with me? Did she know of a Helen Drewmore? If so, why not say so? Still, it was the only lead I had so far, so I definitely intended to follow it up.

While I was in Candlefield, I decided to drop in at Cuppy C. It would be nice to catch up with the two mothers-to-be.

What? No, of course it wasn't only because I wanted a muffin. Sheesh!

"Hi, Jill."

I wasn't sure if it was just my imagination, but Amber looked particularly radiant.

"Can I have a blueberry muffin and a coffee, please?"

"Yes, Jill. I'm feeling very well. Thanks for asking."

"I don't need to ask. I can see you are. You're positively glowing."

"Morning, Jill." Pearl came from out the back.

"Wow! You're both glowing. Pregnancy obviously suits the two of you."

"You should try it." Pearl grinned.

"Two new kids in the family is enough for now. Is there any chance of that muffin? A person could die of starvation."

"Daze is over there. Why don't you join her, and I'll bring it over?" Amber offered.

"Okay, thanks."

"Hi, Daze. Are you by yourself?"

"Yeah. I've left Blaze to clean out the fryer."

"I bet he loves you for that. You're still working at the chip shop, then?"

"Yeah. So far, the gargoyles have been a no-show. I'll give it a few more days, but then we'll have to call it a bust. My clothes stink of fish and chips. Anyway, never mind me and my woes, what about the twins?"

"You've heard, then?"

"Yeah. They've been telling everyone. They're looking good, don't you think?"

"Are you two talking about us?" Amber said, as she and Pearl joined us at the table.

"Daze was just saying how well you both look."

"Thanks, Daze," Pearl said. "I feel great."

"How are you two going to cope with a baby *and* a new dog?" I asked.

"Didn't we tell you? We called Duncan O'Nuts to tell

him that we wouldn't be able to take the puppies. It's a shame, but we need to focus on the babies. We can get puppies for the kids when they're old enough to play with them."

"That's a pity, but it's probably for the best. What did Duncan say?"

"He was very understanding. He said he'd have no difficulty finding homes for the pups."

***

Just as on my previous visit, I'd arranged to arrive at Murray Murray's house a few minutes before his ghostwriter, Lorenzo Woolshape, was due to get there.

"I don't understand what you hope to achieve, Jill?" Murray said. "Surely, if there was anything untoward going on, you would have seen it the last time you hid in the writing room?"

"I believe in being thorough. If I don't uncover anything this time, I think it's safe to assume that Lorenzo is on the level. I'll go and hide in the office."

"Okay. Do you want me to make myself scarce again?"

"Not this time. I'd like you to find an excuse to call Lorenzo out of the writing room, approximately ten minutes before the time he usually wraps things up."

"He told me I should never disturb him when he's writing."

"I don't care what he told you. You have to get him out of that room."

"Why?"

"There isn't time to get into that now — he'll be here any minute. You're just going to have to trust me on this."

"What excuse shall I use?"

"I don't know. Anything. Tell him the house is on fire if you have to. Just make sure you get him out of there."

Fortunately, before Murray could ask any more awkward questions, there was a knock at the door.

"That must be him. You answer the door while I go and hide."

Murray was obviously perplexed, but did as I asked. Meanwhile, I hurried through to the office, and made myself invisible.

A couple of minutes later, Murray showed Lorenzo into the room. Once alone, Lorenzo once again sat back in the chair with his feet on the desk.

The next couple of hours dragged, and it didn't help that I had to put up with Lorenzo's snoring.

When the door opened, Lorenzo almost fell backwards off his chair.

"Murray? I said I wasn't to be disturbed under any circumstances."

"I'm very sorry, but there's a—err—fire. A fire drill. Everyone has to leave the house."

"I didn't hear an alarm?"

"You must have been too busy with your writing. Come on, we have to go now."

Murray was a terrible liar, but Lorenzo was still only half awake, and in no state to argue.

Not long afterwards, the ghost appeared. He looked around, obviously wondering where Lorenzo was.

I reversed the 'invisible' spell. "I'll take that."

"Who are you?" He took a step back. "Where did you come from?"

"My name is Jill Gooder. I've been employed by your

wife to find you. You are Malcolm Aynos, I assume?"

"Yes, but I don't understand. You're not a ghost."

"I'm a witch, but I'm able to travel to GT."

"I think I read about you in Ghost Times."

"Sonya is beside herself with worry."

"I thought she'd be glad to see the back of me; I wouldn't blame her."

"She's been worried sick. Why didn't you let her know where you were?"

"I should have done. I thought once I'd been paid for this assignment, that I'd surprise her with the cash I'd earned."

"It's not the money she wants—it's you. You need to get in touch with her, and you need to do it right now."

"What about this?" He held out the latest chapter of Murray's novel.

"I'll take that."

He pulled away.

"It's okay. Give it to me. I'll make sure Lorenzo gets it."

"Where is he, anyway?"

"He got called away, but don't worry. I'll see that he gets it."

"Okay. If you're sure." He handed over the manuscript.

"Incidentally, Malcolm, how much is he paying you for this?"

"Two hundred pounds for the complete book."

"I see. Okay, off you go! Call Sonya straightaway."

"I will." And with that, he disappeared.

Ten minutes later, Lorenzo came rushing into the room, to find me sitting in the chair with my feet up on the desk.

"You? What are you doing in here?" His gaze darted

around the room—no doubt looking for the 'real' ghost writer.

"Waiting for you."

"You have to leave now. I have work to do."

"A lot of it, apparently. You don't appear to have even started yet."

"It won't take me long to knock up a chapter. Now, if you wouldn't mind leaving?"

"You won't be wanting this, then?" I picked up the manuscript from off the floor.

"Where did you get that?" He tried to snatch it, but I was too quick for him.

"From Malcolm, the 'real' ghost writer."

"Who are you really?"

"That's not important right now. What is important is your answer to the next question. Will you undertake to pay Malcolm half the fee you're being paid by Murray Murray?"

"Half? No! Why should I?"

"Maybe because he's the one who's doing the writing?"

"I can't afford to give him half."

"You can't afford not to. If you don't, I'll tell Murray that you didn't write the manuscript. I'll tell him that you've paid someone else to do it."

"He's not going to believe that a ghost wrote it."

"He doesn't need to. If I tell him that you've paid someone else to write it, it won't matter to Murray who that person is. You know how paranoid he is about keeping this secret. He wants the general public to think he's authored it himself. So, what's it to be? Will you pay Malcolm half, or do I tell Murray Murray?"

"Okay, okay. I'll give him half."

"You better had because I'll be keeping a check on you. Got it?"

"Got it."

"Good." I handed him the manuscript. "Off you go now, and give that to Murray Murray."

A few minutes after Lorenzo had left, Murray came to find me. "Well?"

"You were right. It was a waste of time. Lorenzo is on the level. You have nothing to worry about."

"That's great. Thanks, Jill. I can rest easy now. I was beginning to think that using a ghostwriter had been a huge mistake. You'll send me your bill, I assume?"

"It'll be in the post tonight."

I started for the door, but Murray called me back. "Hold on, Jill. I might need your help again soon on another matter."

"Oh?"

"A few items of silver have gone missing over the last few weeks. Nothing major, but it's a little concerning. I've spoken to the police, so hopefully they'll come up with something, but if they don't, maybe I could give you a shout?"

"Of course. You know where to find me."

"Thanks. I really didn't know what I was taking on when I bought this old building; it's just one expense after another. I noticed a few days ago that some of the ornamental features on the front of the house are missing. They must have been blown off during that recent bad storm we had. It's weird, though, because I never spotted the debris on the ground."

"Ornamental features?"

"Yeah, you know. Those ugly things. What do they call

them?"

"Gargoyles?"

"Yeah. Gargoyles. That's it."

Chapter 17

As I drove back into Washbridge city centre, I reflected on a job well done. Murray Murray would get his manuscript, which had been written not by a ghostwriter, but by an actual ghost. Sonya Anyos' mind would be put at ease once she'd heard from her husband, Malcolm. And he would get fair recompense for the work he was doing, rather than the measly two-hundred pounds that Lorenzo had been planning to pay him.

After parking the car, I made a detour to WashBets where, needless to say, I was greeted by Tonya.

"Can I help you?" She stared at me blankly—not a hint of recognition in her eyes.

"I'd like to see Ryan, please."

"If it's a complaint, you should speak to—"

"Bryan. I know."

"Bryan's left. If it's a complaint, you need to see Dianne."

"It isn't a complaint. I'm a friend of Ryan's. Not his girlfriend. Just a friend. Please tell him it's about Megan."

"Who's Megan?"

"Megan is his girlfriend."

"I thought you weren't his girlfriend."

Surely, no court would convict me if I strangled this woman.

When I eventually got to see Ryan, he was wearing his usual worried expression.

"What have I done this time?"

"It's your parents."

"What about them?"

"Megan thinks you're ashamed to let her meet them. She thinks it's because she used to work as a model."

"That's nonsense. It's just that—"

"I know what it is. I assume they live in Candlefield?"

"That's right. It has nothing to do with being ashamed of Megan. They'd love her; I know they would."

"So why not get them to come over to Washbridge? Couldn't the four of you go out for dinner or something?"

"It's not as easy as that. Neither of them has ever been to the human world. They were terrified for me when I decided to live and work here."

"Well, one thing is for sure: Megan can't go to Candlefield."

"You're in a similar position, aren't you, Jill? How do you handle it?"

"It isn't easy. My relatives do visit us, so that helps, but Jack still asks awkward questions. Sometimes I have no choice but to use the 'forget' spell to take Jack's mind off the subject."

"It's okay for you. I can't just cast a spell."

"I know. All the more reason for you to try to convince your parents to come over to the human world."

"You're right. I'll speak to them tonight. Thanks for doing this, Jill. I sometimes think that you're the only thing keeping our relationship on track."

"That's okay. I just wish I didn't have to get past Tonya every time I come to see you."

"She can be a bit of a bulldog."

I was walking past Ever when someone grabbed my arm, and pulled me inside.

"Grandma? What are you doing?"

"I've been waiting to hear from you."

"About what?"

"The witchfinders, of course. Have you located them yet?"

"No, but then I have been really busy."

"What kind of excuse is that? Finding the witchfinders should be your number one priority. If they catch you off guard, it will be the end of you. Zap! Just like that."

"I know, and I'm being extra vigilant, but I haven't spotted anyone who matches the description that Yvonne gave me."

"Just don't let your guard down. Okay?"

"I promise."

Grandma returned to her office, and I went over to talk to Kathy who had just come down from the roof terrace.

"How's my favourite Everette?"

"Don't start, Jill. I'm not in the mood. There's a cantankerous old man on the roof terrace who makes your grandmother seem reasonable and mild mannered. He just complained that he didn't like the shape of the ice cubes in his cocktail."

"You should have poured it over his head."

"Don't tempt me."

"How's Peter?"

"Alright, why?"

"I bumped into him yesterday, and he just seemed a bit — err — off it."

"Don't tell me — let me guess. He told you about that stupid maze, didn't he?"

"He might have mentioned it."

"It's ridiculous. It's one thing for Lizzie to believe in

ghosts, but I'm not standing for it from Pete. He was absolutely terrified when he called me yesterday morning. He'd walked off the job because he reckoned he'd seen a ghost with its head under its arm. I told him not to be so silly. Anyway, when he came home last night, he'd been back to finish the job, and guess what?"

"No ghosts?"

"Got it in one. That man does my head in sometimes. How are things with you? Busy?"

"Yeah. I've got work coming at me from all angles. Oh, and I have some big news."

"You're pregnant?"

"No, but the twins are."

"Which one of them?"

"Both of them."

"That's fantastic! You'll have to get them to come over sometime. Or we could go and visit them. That would make a nice change."

"I'll speak to them, and see what I can arrange. Better rush. Bye."

***

When I was halfway up the stairs to my offices, I heard the sound of someone crying.

"Jules? Whatever is the matter?"

"It's Gilbert," she managed, but then the waterworks really started.

"Why don't I make you a nice cup of tea, and then you can tell me all about it?"

What? I can do sympathetic. Or, at least, what passes as a good impression of it.

"There you go." I passed her the tea, and waited until she'd dried her eyes and wiped her runny nose. "What's happened?"

"He's found someone else."

"Are you sure? He seemed so fond of you."

"I'm positive. It's all the fault of those stupid bottle tops."

"How do you mean?"

"We were fine together before he became interested in those. When we were at ToppersCon, I saw him talking to this one girl a few times. I didn't think anything of it at the time, but then yesterday, I saw what was on his phone."

"Why were you looking at his phone?"

"Because I sensed he was up to something behind my back. There were tons of messages from that girl. And pictures of her blowing kisses to him."

"What did you do?"

"I confronted him about it."

"What did he say?"

"That he thought we should call it a day."

"I'm really sorry, Jules. That's horrible."

"I wouldn't mind so much, but he said the reason he was chucking me was because she was into bottle tops. He said he couldn't talk to me about them. It isn't fair, Jill." She started to cry again. "I've been dumped for bottle tops."

"He isn't worth it, Jules. There are plenty more fish in the sea. Look, why don't you call it a day, and go home?"

"Are you sure?"

"Yeah. You get off. And you should go out tonight with your friends. You'll soon forget about—err—what's-his-name."

"What's that awful noise out there?" Winky asked when I went through to my office.

"It's just Jules. She's upset. Her boyfriend has just dumped her over bottle tops."

"You humans are weird."

"Who are you calling human? And how come you aren't busy making your silly tin foil hats?"

"I would be, but I have a tin foil emergency."

"How come?"

"I've run out."

"The answer's no."

"What are you talking about?"

"I assume you were about to ask me to go and buy some tin foil for you. Well, the answer is no. I'm too busy."

"There's no need. It's already in hand."

Just then, there was a knock at my office door.

"Hi." The young man was dressed in a very smart, blue uniform and matching cap.

"Can I help you?"

"I have a delivery." He passed me a note to sign.

"Express Tin Foil?"

"I have three rolls downstairs. Is it okay if I bring them up?"

I glanced at Winky who was all smiles.

"Yes. I suppose so."

"Great. It's cash on delivery, as arranged."

"Hold on! What?" It was too late; he was already on his way downstairs.

I had no choice but to pay, but as soon as the delivery man had left, I grabbed Winky, tipped him upside down, and shook him until I had my money back.

And before you write in to complain, I didn't literally tip him upside down and shake him. Sheesh, what do you think I am? Don't answer that.

***

I had two stops to make on the way home: the corner shop, and first, the fish and chip shop where I found Daze and Blaze hard at work. They looked equally miserable.

"Hi, guys. It's always good to see people happy in their work."

They both shot me the same withering look.

"I hate this assignment," Blaze leaned on the counter. "Maze has threatened to dump me if I keep coming home smelling of fish."

"I have something to tell you which will enable you to get out of here."

"I'm listening," Daze said.

"I think you may be looking in the wrong place for your gargoyles."

"How so?"

"I've been working on a case at Colonel Briggs' old house."

"Didn't a popstar buy that place?"

"Yes. Murray Murray owns it now. Anyway, while I was up there, Murray happened to mention that a few small items of silver had gone missing. He also said that some of the gargoyles had disappeared off the front of the building. He assumed they'd been blown off during the recent storms."

"Jill!" Daze beamed. "You're a life-saver."

"Don't get your hopes up too high. I'm only telling you what Murray told me."

"Come on, Blaze." Daze was already taking off her smock. "We have work to do."

He didn't need telling twice.

"What about the customers?" I asked.

"They'll just have to manage without their fish and chips for one day. We have bigger gargoyles to fry. Thanks, Jill."

Tish and Chip wouldn't be very thrilled when they discovered that they'd lost an evening's takings, but at least Daze and Blaze were happy. Hopefully, they'd catch the gargoyles, and maybe even recover Murray Murray's silver.

When I arrived at the corner shop, there was no sign of the string that had obstructed the aisles on my previous visit. As I picked up the few bits and pieces I needed, I noticed that several mirrors had been stuck to the walls at regular intervals.

"Good day, Jill." Little Jack Corner greeted me.

"Hi, Jack. I see you've given up on the hydraulic platform."

"Yes. I sent it back for a refund. The last time I tried it, I almost decapitated myself. I had to jump off, onto a pile of toilet rolls."

"Gosh. Were you okay?"

"Yes. Fortunately, they were the luxury brand. Double cushioned."

"I couldn't help but notice that you've put up lots of mirrors?"

"That's Cornercomms mark two."

"Sorry?"

"You may recall that the last time you were in here, we were using the cans and string to communicate with one another."

"I do indeed. We had to limbo under the string."

"We had a few complaints about that. The truth is that Cornercomms mark one hadn't been given enough thought. We've now scrapped that idea, and replaced it with mark two."

"The mirrors?"

"Precisely."

"And how exactly does Cornercomms mark two work?"

"Would you like to see a demonstration?"

"Sure."

He reached under the counter, and produced a hand torch.

"Depending on where Missy is in the shop, I shine this torch at the appropriate mirror. So, for example, if she was in the biscuit aisle, I would shine it at the first mirror over there. At the moment, she's actually at the far end of the shop —"

"Near the buckets?"

"That's right, so I'll shine it at the third mirror. Watch. I'll show you."

He pointed the torch at the third mirror, and flashed it on and off. A few moments later, the light from Missy's torch could be seen in that same mirror.

"Semaphore, I assume?"

"Exactly. And the beauty of Cornercomms mark two is that there's no string to obstruct the aisles."

"Quite ingenious."

"Thank you. Would you like me to signal Missy to bring you a bucket while she's down there?"

"No, thanks. I'm still good for buckets."

When I arrived home, Jack was already in the house.

"Where did you buy those?" I pointed to the plateful of cupcakes.

"I didn't. Blossom brought them over a few minutes ago."

"That was nice of her."

"Apparently, she's just heard she's going to be a great-grandma. She bought these to celebrate. She was so excited."

"Bless. Blossom is lovely."

"Which is more than can be said for those two weirdos who have moved in next door to her."

"Have you actually managed to speak to them properly yet?"

"No. They were getting into their van when I got home; they were wearing matching balaclavas again. I waved to them, and shouted 'hi', but they just ignored me, and drove off. Have you noticed that all the windows in their van are tinted?"

"Oh well. At least we have one nice new neighbour. Let's see what we have here. By my calculations, that's three cupcakes for me, and two for you."

Chapter 18

When I arrived at the office the next morning, Mrs V was by herself.

"Morning, Mrs V. Not knitting?"

"I'm too nervous to knit, dear."

"Nervous about what?"

"The competition on Saturday, of course."

"You don't have anything to be nervous about. I've told Jack he has to let you and Armi win."

"No!" She looked horrified. "He mustn't do that. I wouldn't want to win by underhand means."

What was wrong with people?

"Relax. I'm only joking. And, besides, Jack would never agree to do anything like that."

"Of course he wouldn't. A man of integrity is Jack."

"Just like me."

"Hmm?"

"How is the practising going?"

"Really well. Armi and I seem to have hit our peak at just the right time."

"It should be in the bag, then?"

"Hopefully, but you should never count your chickens. Do you remember when Armi broke his ankle just before the Cuckoo Clock Appreciation Society dinner and dance?"

"That was really unlucky."

"I've warned him to be extra careful because if he does it again, I'll break his other leg. Anyway, enough about me. How was your visit to Jack's parents?"

"We had a lovely weekend, thanks. I won at Monopoly."

"I hope you didn't cheat."

"Of course not. And I got to see photos of Jack when he was a baby. He wasn't best pleased about that."

"What are mothers for if not to embarrass you?"

"While I think of it, I'd better warn you to be gentle with Jules when you see her next."

"Why? What's the matter?"

"She and Gilbert have split up. Or to be more precise, he's dumped her for a woman who shares his passion for bottle tops."

"Poor girl."

***

Once again, there was a long queue of cats, all waiting to purchase Winky's tin foil hats. I couldn't get my head around why there would be so much demand for them.

"Excuse me," I said to the Russian Blue at the back of the queue.

"Yes?"

"I'm curious about what prompted you to buy a tin foil hat today?"

"Haven't you seen the news article?"

"I can't say I have."

He produced a phone, and brought up a video. It was a feline news article filmed out on the streets of Washbridge. The reporter was a cat, wearing sunglasses and a large brimmed hat. I held it close to my ear, so I could hear what was being said.

Reports are still coming in of UFOs spotted in the sky above Washbridge. The authorities are advising everyone to take cover inside, but first, as a matter of urgency, you must obtain the only protection available: a tin foil hat.

I was just about to hand back the phone when I noticed the small strip across the bottom of the video; on it was a scrolling message: ***Sponsored by Winky's Tin Foil Hats.***

"Thanks." I handed back the phone.

Just then, my phone rang. It was Desmond Sidings.

"Miss Gooder, the police have confirmed that they're going to hand back The Flyer this afternoon if you still want to take a look around the old girl."

"Definitely. I'll come over early afternoon."

Meanwhile, more and more cats were coming through the window to join the queue for tin foil hats.

***

I magicked myself over to Candlefield, and made my way to the house where Cynthia Drewmore lived.

"Cynthia. I spoke to you yesterday."

"Come in." She was very business-like. "Let's go through to the living room."

"Thank you for seeing me."

"What's this all about?"

"Like I said on the phone. I'm trying to trace descendants of a Helen Drewmore."

"I know that. But why?"

"It's rather difficult to explain."

"Try. I don't have much time to spare."

"Okay. Well, I guess it all started with this locket." I opened it for her to see. "I've been trying to find out who these two people are."

She stared at it, and then back at me. "Where did you get this?"

"The man in the picture left it in my office. At least, I think he did; I didn't actually see him do it. He was found dead the same day."

"He's dead?" The colour drained from her face, and I thought she might collapse.

"Are you okay?"

"Yes." She didn't look it. "Are you sure he's dead?"

"Positive. I realise that I'm not making much sense. Maybe it would help if I told you why I'm looking for Helen Drewmore?"

"Okay."

"Have you heard of CASS?"

"The school? Of course."

"I visited there some time ago, and while I was there I had a feeling that I somehow had a connection to the place. I was drawn to one room in particular. It was in there that I saw the two people in this locket. Helen Drewmore was there too."

"You can't have seen Helen." Cynthia blurted out.

"So, you do know her?"

"I know you can't possibly have seen her."

"When I say that I saw her, she wasn't actually there — none of them were. I think it was some kind of distant memory. I heard them talking, and then I saw the young woman hand this locket to Helen. This must sound like nonsense to you?"

Cynthia took a seat, and for the first time, her stony face cracked — just a little. "Actually, it doesn't."

"It doesn't?"

"I heard about the locket, and the two people whose

portraits are in it from my mother. She was told the story by *her* mother — my grandmother: Helen Drewmore."

"But if your mother married, how come —?"

"She kept the name Drewmore, and passed it on to me? Because my grandmother asked us to keep the name, so that we could be found when the time came."

"Found by who? By me?"

"Yes, but not only you. There was someone who came before you — before I was born. Her name was — "

"Magna Mondale?"

"That's right. I think I should make us a drink. This is a long story."

After she'd made tea, I joined her on the sofa. Her whole demeanour had changed, and she now seemed keen to help.

"My grandmother, Helen, was initially employed as Juliet Braxmore's nanny, and then later, she became her handmaid and companion."

"Braxmore?"

"You've heard the name before?"

"Yes. Wasn't he one of the most powerful wizards in Candlefield?"

"Back then, they were known as grandmasters. There were two of them: Braxmore and Charles Wrongacre."

"The building where CASS is now housed used to belong to Wrongacre."

"That's right. The red-haired man in the locket is his son, Damon. Wrongacre was a good man, but Braxmore was evil personified. He may still be."

"He's still alive, after all this time?"

"No one knows for sure, but there have been rumours.

Anyway, as I was saying, Juliet was Braxmore's daughter. Unlike her father, she was loving and kind. She and Damon fell in love, and wanted to marry, but Braxmore wouldn't allow it. Rather than be separated, Juliet and Damon died together."

"They committed suicide?"

"Not exactly. It's much more complicated than that, but it's all explained in my grandmother's journal."

"Do you have it?"

"Yes. On her deathbed, my grandmother gave it to my mother, Freda. She, in turn, gave it to me, just before she passed away. Just as my mother had done, I promised never to show it to another living soul until—"

"Until what?"

"Until either one of the two people whose portraits appear in the locket showed up at our door. My grandmother said that they would come to claim the locket one day. Look, it's very complicated, but the journal makes it all much clearer."

"Can I see it?"

"You don't look like the woman in the locket, but you can only have got it from one person: the red-bearded man. I'm happy for you to see the journal, but I'd rather you took it away with you. I've now fulfilled my obligation to my mother and grandmother. To tell you the truth, I'll be glad to be rid of it."

***

After leaving Cynthia's house, I wandered around, in something of a daze.

"Jill!" someone shouted.

It took me a few seconds to realise that it was Aunt Lucy. She had Barry with her; he was straining at the lead, trying to get across the road to me.

"Hi, you two." As soon as I reached them, Barry jumped up and planted his front paws on my chest. "Get down, you big, soft lump."

"We're going to the park!" He was as excited as ever. "We're going to see Babs!"

"That's great."

"I've arranged to meet Dolly." Aunt Lucy pulled Barry off me. "Why don't you come with us?"

"I'm sorry, but I can't."

"Please, Jill!" Barry pleaded.

"I'd like to, big guy, but I'm really busy. You'll have a great time with Babs. You don't need me there."

"What's the book?" Aunt Lucy pointed to the journal in my hand.

"This? It's—err—nothing. Just a case I'm working on."

"I know you said you're busy, Jill, but Hamlet did ask me to tell you it's very urgent that he speaks with you."

"Okay. I'll pop in to see him, and then I really must get back to Washbridge. Enjoy the park, Barry."

"I will. I love the park. I love to play with Babs."

"Bye, then."

Aunt Lucy tried to wave, but she was practically pulled off her feet, as Barry took off down the road.

As always, Aunt Lucy's house wasn't locked, so I let myself in, and went to see what the hamster emergency was all about.

"Not before time!" Hamlet sighed. It struck me that he and Grandma had a lot in common.

"I came as soon as I knew you wanted to see me. What's the problem?"

"That soft dog of yours is the problem."

"I thought you and Barry were getting along okay now."

"I can just about put up with that stupid canine; it's his fleas that I take exception to."

"Barry doesn't have fleas. Aunt Lucy would have mentioned it."

"She doesn't have to share the same room as him." He picked at the soft fur on his underside, and produced a flea. "Look!"

"Oh dear. And you're sure they came from Barry?"

"You're surely not suggesting *I* brought them into the house?"

"Err—no, of course not. I suppose I'd better buy some flea powder."

"You better had, and quickly, otherwise the whole house will be infested."

"Okay, I'm on it."

I checked Candlefield Pages and discovered there was a pet shop, called Pets-A-GoGo, not far from Aunt Lucy's house. As I made my way there, I was scratching my arms and legs non-stop. I couldn't see any fleas; hopefully, it was just my imagination working overtime.

The notice on the door of Pets-A-GoGo read: No Animals Allowed.

Inside, the shop was deserted except for the funny little wizard behind the counter; he had a definite look of a squirrel about him—probably on account of his puffed-out cheeks.

"Hi!" I said, trying to ignore my itchy arm.

"Hello." He scowled.

"It's very quiet in here."

"It always is. I hate this place."

"Oh? Have you worked here long?"

"I own the shop. I'm Hugh. Hugh Mann."

"Nice to meet you, Hugh. I'm Jill. Isn't it rather unusual for a pet shop not to allow animals inside?"

"I can't stand them."

"Sorry?"

"Animals. I can't stand the smelly, horrible things."

"Any in particular?"

"All of them."

"This may be a silly question, but why would you run a pet shop if you don't like animals?"

"It was my parents' shop. They're dead now."

"I'm sorry."

"Me too. They landed me with this awful place. I'm thinking of going into another line of business. I hear nail bars can be quite profitable. What do you think?"

"I'm not really the person to ask, but they do seem to be popping up everywhere."

"You don't get smelly animals in nail bars."

"That's true. Anyway, the reason I'm here is to buy some flea powder for my dog."

Hugh took two steps back from the counter. "Do you have fleas?"

"No, of course not." I scratched the back of my hand.

"Are you sure?"

"Positive."

"The flea powder is down that aisle, on the top shelf. Leave the cash on the floor, would you? I'll pick it up after

you've gone."
    Charming.

Chapter 19

I took the flea powder back to Aunt Lucy's house. Once there, while I waited for Barry to come back from the park, I took a look at the journal that Cynthia Drewmore had given to me. The scribblings, and that's what they were, weren't easy to decipher, but I persevered, and slowly but surely, the story started to emerge.

Juliet Braxmore was indeed the daughter of one of the most powerful, but evil wizards that Candlefield had ever known. After Juliet's mother had died in childbirth, Helen was employed as nanny. Braxmore had very little to do with raising his daughter, preferring to leave it to Helen. It was obvious from her writing that Helen looked upon Juliet as her own daughter, and that Juliet thought of Helen as a surrogate mother. Helen offered to leave her employ once Juliet reached adulthood, but Juliet wouldn't hear of it, so Helen stayed on as her handmaid and companion.

Damon was the son of Charles Wrongacre. The details of how Juliet and Damon met were sketchy, but one thing was very clear: Braxmore did not approve of the union. He demanded that Juliet have nothing further to do with Damon, and threatened to kill him if she persisted in the relationship. The two young people could not bear the thought of being apart, but knew that to stay together would result in Damon's death. In desperation, they turned to Damon's father, Charles Wrongacre, who had always been supportive of their relationship.

His proposed solution was radical and extremely shocking.

Wrongacre rightly concluded that Braxmore would never allow the relationship, and that he would rather the couple were dead than together. In desperation, Wrongacre proposed that he would create a spell that would 'kill' Juliet and Damon, but which would then allow them to return from the dead many years later. No one had ever created such a spell before, and so it was with much trepidation that the young couple agreed to the plan.

When it was time to cast the spell, Wrongacre told the couple that they would both return not once, but twice. The reason for that, he explained, was that he could not be sure how long Braxmore would live. Should he still be alive on their first return, he would no doubt do everything in his power to track them down and destroy them. If that happened, they would still have another chance to find happiness together.

It was clear from Helen's writing that she had been very nervous about the plan, and had tried desperately hard to talk Juliet out of it. But Juliet had said that without Damon, she might as well be dead anyway. Helen had not been present when the spells were cast; Juliet had insisted she leave, and take with her a locket that contained pictures of the two lovers.

The next thing Helen had heard was when the deaths of the two young people were announced. She sought out Wrongacre who was beside himself with grief. He had not had sufficient time to perfect the spell, but had been forced to proceed anyway. To have waited any longer would have meant certain death for Damon. Juliet had wanted Wrongacre to cast the spell on her first, but Damon insisted it must be him—that way, if for any reason it failed, Juliet need not subject herself to it. As it turned out, the spell went without a hitch on Damon, but there were problems when Wrongacre came to cast the spell on Juliet. Braxmore's men were at the doors, and managed to break through before Wrongacre had finished. Through tears of despair, he told Helen that he didn't think the spell had worked fully on Juliet. Either way, the two young people were pronounced 'dead', and were buried in separate graves on their own estates because Braxmore would not entertain the idea of their being laid to rest together.

The next entry simply read:
Wherever Juliet and Damon are, I pray they find the happiness they so deserve.

The next entry, which was dated many years later, was in a different handwriting. It read:
Helen Drewmore, my mother, died two days ago. She made me promise that I would keep up this journal. Even on her deathbed, she still believed that Juliet and Damon would return one day. I didn't have the heart to tell her that there is now little likelihood of that.
Freda Drewmore.

The next entry, which was again in Freda Drewmore's handwriting read:
Damon has returned! I recognised him immediately from his picture in the locket. We talked for some time — he told me that he had only recently realised who he was. Until a few weeks ago, he had lived under the name of Thomas, but then his memory had returned. He first remembered his name, and then he remembered Juliet, the love of his life. He told me that he

thought he may have tracked her down, but that she looked different, and wasn't living under the name of Juliet. The woman, named Magna, did not appear to have any memory of him or her previous life. He asked if he could take the locket, in the hope that it might jog the woman's memory. I pray that it does, and that they will be re-united.

A few days later, there was another entry:

A woman by the name of Magna Mondale came to my door today. She had the locket that I had given to Damon. She seemed both confused and upset. Confused by the story that Damon had told her because she had no memory of him or of anyone named Juliet. And upset because the day after he had visited her, he was found dead. Damon had told her of my family's connection, so Magna had decided to return the locket to me. Even though she did not look like the woman in the locket, I felt that she must be Juliet, so I offered to let her read the journal. She declined because she was sure Damon had got the wrong person.

The next entry in the journal was dated two days later:

I have just heard that Magna Mondale is dead.

The final entry in the journal was in yet another person's handwriting. This one was dated only a few months earlier.

Damon is back. He told me that he had been living under the name of Henry until a few weeks ago when his memories began to return. He has been searching for Juliet, and thinks he may have found her, although she does not look like the portrait in the locket. The woman's name is Jill, but he fears she has no memories of him or their former life together. He has taken the locket which he intends to give to her in the hope it will jog her memory.

I pray that it works this time.
Cynthia Drewmore.

No wonder Cynthia had been so upset when I'd told her that I'd found Damon dead.

Just then, I heard the front door open, and the sound of footsteps. Aunt Lucy and Barry were back, so I quickly slid the journal into my bag.

"Jill? I didn't expect to find you still here." Aunt Lucy looked red in the face, and sounded a little out of breath.

"Has he run you ragged?"

"As always."

"Can I have a quiet word?"

"Of course. Upstairs, you go, Barry." She gave him a gentle tap on the bottom, and he ran off up the stairs. "What is it?"

"It seems Barry has fleas." I took the powder out of my bag.

"Are you sure?" She began to scratch her arms. "I haven't seen any."

"Hamlet told me. I'm going to treat Barry with the powder while he's still tired from his walk."

"Good luck with that."

"Hi, Barry."

"Hi." He was flat-out on the floor.

"Pssst!" Hamlet beckoned to me. "Did you get it?"

I gave him the thumbs up.

"Just stay still boy while I —"

Barry spotted the flea powder in my hand, and jumped to his feet. "What's that?"

"It's nothing to worry about. It's just flea powder."

"I don't have fleas!"

"You do, but this will get rid of them."

"I don't like flea powder. Take it away."

"It won't hurt you. Just stand still for a few minutes." I had him backed up against the cupboard. "I'm just going to sprinkle this—"

He shot through my legs, and out of the door, but not before I'd overbalanced and emptied most of the contents.

All over Hamlet's cage.

"Achoo!" Hamlet sneezed. He was covered, head to toe, in the powder.

"Sorry, Hamlet."

"That's just great!" He shook himself.

"It was an accident. Sorry, but I—err—I have to go. Urgent appointment. Bye!"

***

As I magicked myself back to Washbridge, my head was still spinning with thoughts of Helen Drewmore's journal. Sooner or later, I'd have to try to work out what it all meant, but for now, I had to focus on the Washbridge Flyer murders.

I'd arranged to meet Desmond Sidings at the station.

"Would you like to start with the engine?" he asked. "That's the most interesting part."

"No offence, but I'm not really into steam trains. I'm only interested in seeing the carriages where the murders took place."

"Fair enough. Follow me."

He led the way onto the platform where the Washbridge Flyer was standing. Even though I'm not a train buff, I could appreciate what an amazing piece of engineering it was. The engine and carriages were in pristine condition—from the outside at least.

"Let's start with the front carriage." He climbed aboard.

I was very impressed. Unlike all the trains I'd ever travelled on, this one had class—a touch of elegance if you will. The seats had obviously been re-upholstered, and all the wooden surfaces and the metalwork were polished to a shine. On one side of the central aisle were tables with four seats. On the opposite side were individual seats.

"The Shores were seated there." Desmond pointed to a table in the centre of the carriage.

"Where's the toilet where Gena Shore's body was found?"

"Through that door." He pointed.

I walked the length of the carriage, and went through the door. The toilet was on the left, and in front of me, another door.

"I take it that the buffet car is through there?"

"Correct."

I glanced back and forth. "This area isn't visible from either the front carriage or the buffet car, is it?"

"No. Unlike most modern trains, there isn't glass in the doors between carriages."

Just beyond the toilet, there were two external doors; one on either side of the carriage.

"I assume that Gary Shore jumped, or was pushed through one of these?"

"That's right. It would have been that one." He pointed.

I took a quick look around, and then suggested we

move on through to the buffet car, which was a shorter carriage than the first one. The shutter on the serving hatch was down.

"I was expecting something grander."

"In its heyday, The Flyer had a buffet car with a fully fitted kitchen, but we would never be able to recover the costs of running that today, so we have to make do with this. Shall we continue?" He led the way to the far end of the buffet car, and through the door to the rear carriage.

Once again, we found ourselves in a small corridor with a toilet—identical to that in the front carriage.

"This is where Carol Strand was found, I assume?"

"That's right." He led the way into the seated area of the rear carriage; it was identical to the first one we'd seen.

"What's through there?" I pointed to a door at the far end.

"That would normally be the guard's van, but these days it's only used for storage: food, toilet rolls, that sort of thing.

"Can I see inside?"

"I'm sorry. I didn't think to bring the key."

"Is it normally open during the weekly trips?"

"No. The passengers aren't allowed in there. Only the guards have a key, so they can get any supplies they might need."

"Okay, this has been very informative, but what would really help is if I was able to go on your next trip. Would that be possible?"

"Of course. The police have given us the green light, so The Flyer will run this Sunday as usual."

"Great. I'll be there."

As soon as we stepped off the train, we were approached by a woman with a microphone, and a man with a camera.

"Mr Sidings." The woman with the mic blocked our way. "We understand that you plan to run the Washbridge Flyer as usual this Sunday. Isn't that rather reckless given that the murders are still unsolved?"

"Not at all." Desmond Sidings was remarkably calm under the circumstances. "The police have given us the all-clear, and that's good enough for me. There's no reason to suspect that there will be any further issues."

"*Issues?*" The woman sounded as outraged as it was possible to sound. "Is that what you call multiple murders?"

That was my cue to slip away. He would have to handle this one on his own.

Chapter 20

"I'm beginning to think that sandpit of yours was not such a great idea," Jack said, while eating his muesli, and staring out of the kitchen window.

"You agreed it would be good for when the kids came around."

"I know, but over the last couple of days I've noticed paw prints in the sand. I hope the local cats haven't decided it's a huge litter tray."

"They'd better not have!" I joined him at the window.

"Look, over there."

Oh bum! Those weren't cat paw prints; they were too square.

"It'll probably be okay. We'll see how it goes."

Jack finished his muesli, put the dish in the sink, and then went through to the lounge, where I heard him switch on the early morning TV news. While he was engrossed in that, I slipped outside.

"Joey! Hey, Joey!"

"Who's Joey?" Megan was standing next to her dustbin.

"Joey? Err—he's—err—a budgie."

"I didn't know you had a budgie."

"It's Jack's, actually. He's always kept budgies, ever since he was a kid."

"What's it doing outside?"

"I didn't realise it was out of its cage, and I opened the back door."

"Oh dear. He could be anywhere by now."

"He won't go far. He's done this before."

"I could help you look."

"No, that's alright. He'll turn up."

"Okay, and by the way, I have some good news. Ryan's parents are coming over for dinner at my house next week."

"That's great. I told you there was nothing to worry about."

"I know. I feel silly for getting so worked up about it. And now, I'm really nervous about meeting them."

Not as nervous as they're going to be on their first trip to the human world. "I'm sure everything will be fine. They're bound to love you."

"That's sweet of you to say. Are you sure you wouldn't like me to help you to find Joey?"

"No, it's fine. Thanks, anyway."

I waited until Megan was inside her house, and then tried again, "Joey!"

"Is the coast clear?" The tiny sand sloth popped his head out.

"Yes, but be ready to disappear if Jack comes out."

"Okay."

"You've got to be more careful about leaving footprints in the sand."

"Whoops! Sorry."

"*Sorry* doesn't cut it. Jack thinks all the neighbourhood cats are using the sandpit as their litter tray."

"A few of them have tried to, but I ran them off. That's why my footprints are everywhere."

"I appreciate you keeping the cats away, but you really will have to clean up your own footprints, otherwise Jack may decide to get rid of the sandpit. You wouldn't want that, would you?"

"Definitely not. I'll be more careful in future."

When I got back in the house, Jack called to me, "You're on the TV."

Sure enough, there I was, standing next to Desmond Sidings. It hadn't occurred to me that they might have caught me on camera.

"They got your good side." Jack grinned.

"What do you mean, *good side*?" I checked the mirror. "Are you saying I have a bad side?"

"Of course not." He gave me a peck on the cheek. "Both of your sides are equally beautiful."

Back on the TV, the interview with Desmond Sidings was over, but they were still covering the Washbridge Flyer story. On screen now, was a man, standing in front of a block of flats. According to the caption at the bottom of the screen, the man was Thomas West, the guard who had been on the first Flyer trip. If I remembered correctly, he'd handed in his notice shortly after that.

"What exactly did you see?" the female interviewer asked.

"I saw Mr and Mrs Shore in the front carriage before the train left the platform. They looked as though they were celebrating something."

"Are you sure about that?" the interviewer pressed. "There's been some speculation that Mr Shore may have murdered his wife, and then committed suicide?"

"I can only tell you what I saw. They seemed perfectly happy together."

"Did you see anything at all that gave you cause for concern?"

"No, but then I was busy serving food in the buffet car for the whole of the journey. The first I knew that something was wrong was when the body was discovered near to the toilet."

"I understand that you resigned after that first trip?"

"That's right. It upset and scared me a great deal. And, after what happened on the second trip, I'm glad I did. I could have been the murderer's next victim."

"Have you spoken to that guard?" Jack asked, after the reporter had handed back to the studio.

"Not yet, but he's next on my list."

***

As I walked from the car to my office, I noticed that the headlines on several of the national newspapers were related to the Washbridge Flyer murders. That surprised me for a couple of reasons: First, they seemed a little late to the game because it was now several days since the second murder. And just as odd: why would the nationals cover the story at all? I quickly skimmed several of the articles, and then all became clear. They had all picked up on the 'serial killer on train' angle. One thing that all the articles had in common was that they all featured interviews with the guard, Thomas West.

***

What a contrast! Jules looked so much happier than the last time I'd seen her.

"Morning, Jill." She beamed. "Isn't it a wonderful day?"

"I'll let you know when I'm awake. I take it that you and Gilbert have made up?"

"Gilbert?" She pulled a face as though she'd just bitten on a lemon. "That wimp is history. I don't know what I ever saw in him and his stupid bottle tops."

"How come you're looking so pleased with life, then?"

"I have Lules to thank, really. It was her idea. I would never have dreamed of using a dating app, but she said I had nothing to lose. And bingo!"

"Bingo?"

"I've got a date."

"I don't want to rain on your parade, but are you sure about this? Online dating can be a bit dodgy."

"This one seems to be perfectly legit. I'm meeting him for lunch today."

"I guess a lunch date should be safe enough, and it will give you a chance to make sure he isn't some kind of monster."

"He's a hunk, Jill. A real man—not like that wimp, Gilbert." She took out her phone, and brought up a photo. "See what I mean?"

I did. The guy was ripped, and then some. He was very good looking too. "WARMA? What's that?"

"That's the name of the app. It stands for Where All the Real Men Are. Clever, eh?"

"I guess. I'm just glad to see you happy again. I hope your lunch date goes well. You don't need to hurry back."

"Thanks, Jill."

When I went through to my office, Winky was fast asleep on the sofa. The pile of tin foil hats had disappeared; he'd sold the lot. What an accomplished conman that cat was.

While he was asleep, I tiptoed over to the sofa, crouched down, and felt underneath.

Eureka! Just as I'd expected.

Just then, Jules came through the door.

"Have you lost something, Jill?"

"Err—I—err—no. I was just checking for dust."

"Oh? Okay. Your accountant is here; he has a woman with him. He wondered if you could spare them a moment."

"Sure. Just give me one minute, and then send them through."

I dusted myself down, and slipped the 'evidence' into the bottom drawer of my desk.

"Luther, Maria, this is unexpected."

"I'm sorry to turn up like this," Luther said. "I just wanted to tell you my big news."

"Are you two getting married?"

"What? No, of course not."

Maria pinned him with a glare.

"Not that there would be anything wrong with that." He backtracked. "It's—err—just not why we're here."

"He won the award," Maria said.

"The Accountant of the Year?"

"Yes." Luther looked like the cat who had got the cream. "I still can't quite believe it."

"Fully deserved, I'm sure. Where did Seymour Sums come?"

"Third, so even if I'd been a no-show, he still wouldn't have won."

"You two will no doubt be celebrating, then?"

"We're going out for dinner tonight. Why don't you and Jack join us?"

"Thanks, but we've already got something planned," I lied. "I guess this means you'll be putting up your hourly rate now?"

"For new clients, yes, but not for my existing customer base, and definitely not for you. In fact, I'm going to give you a twenty-five percent discount for the next twelve months by way of a thank you."

"That's very generous of you."

"The award is good news for me, too," Maria said. "Luther reckons he'll need more clerical and admin assistance to cope with the increase in business he's expecting. He's asked me to work for him."

"But what about the red trouser suit? Won't you miss that?"

She laughed. "I'm going to burn that thing when I leave."

"I wouldn't do that. Grandma will charge you for it."

"It's your sister I feel sorry for. She's already run off her feet."

"Does she know you're leaving yet?"

"No. I'm going to hand in my notice next week."

"Thanks for the tip-off. I'll give Kathy a wide berth for a few days."

By the time Luther and Maria left, Winky was awake—or at least, half-awake.

"How's a cat supposed to sleep with all this noise going on?"

"This is my office."

"Couldn't you have talked to them out front? You could see I was asleep."

"No, I couldn't, Mr Conman."

"Who are you calling a conman?"

"I don't see anyone else in the room."

"That's slander."

"I don't think so." I took the hat and sunglasses out of my drawer, and put them on. Then, using my best Winky impersonation, I shouted, "The aliens are coming. Run for your lives."

The door to my office flew open, and Jules rushed inside. "Jill? Are you alright?"

Oh bum! I'd got carried away, and shouted much louder than I'd intended.

"Yes, thanks, Jules. I'm fine."

"You were shouting something about aliens. And, why are you wearing that hat, and those sunglasses?"

"Oh? I—err—I was just practising my lines."

"Lines for what?"

"The—err—amateur dramatics production that my sister has signed me up for."

"Really? What's the play?"

"It's—err—The Unexpected Guest."

"What part do you play?"

"The inspector."

"Let me know when it is. Me and Lules will come and support you."

Oh bum!

"You are unbelievable," Winky said, after Jules had gone back to her office. "Lies just come tumbling out of your mouth, don't they?"

"That's rich coming from you."

"At least my lies earn me money. All you ever manage to do is dig yourself into yet another hole."

"Jules will have forgotten about this by the end of the week. She has much more important things on her mind. Anyway, was the tin foil hat con worth it? Do you have enough cash to pay back Big Gordy what you owe him?"

"Almost, and I'm sure I'll be able to scrape up the rest before he comes to collect. Now, can I have my hat and sunglasses back, please?"

Chapter 21

I'd told Jules that she could have a long lunch, and she'd certainly taken me at my word because it was just under two hours since she'd left the office. Normally I wouldn't have minded, but I couldn't for the life of me figure out where she kept the staples.

I was in the outer office, going through the desk drawers when I heard Jules' voice on the stairs; she was chatting and giggling with someone.

"Sorry, Jill. I didn't mean to stay out this long. This is Dexter." The young man who followed her into the office was even bigger in real life than he'd looked in his photograph. He was a man-mountain, and there was one very obvious reason for that—obvious to me, at least.

He was a werewolf.

"Hi." Dexter stepped forward, and shook my hand. His grip was so strong, I thought he was going to crush it.

"Dexter asked if he could see where I worked," Jules said. "I hope you don't mind?"

"Not at all."

"Were you looking for something, Jill?" Jules asked.

"Nothing important." I started back to my office, but then hesitated. "Dexter. I could use some help to move something. Would you have a minute to lend me a hand?"

"Yes, of course."

He followed me through to my office, and I pushed the door closed behind us. I'd have to make this quick otherwise Jules might think I was making a pass at her new boyfriend.

"What's your game, Buster?" I said, in a hushed, but hopefully threatening, tone.

He took a step back; he obviously hadn't encountered a crazy witch before.

"Nothing. Honestly."

"Jules works for me, and I'm very protective of my staff. Do you understand?"

"Yes, of course."

"Why are you over here, dating humans?"

"This is my first time."

"What's going to happen when it's the full moon?"

"I'll go back to the Range in Candlefield."

"You better had. If you harm one hair on Jules' head, you'll have me to answer to. Got it?"

"Got it."

"Good. Now, off you trot, and just know that I have eyes everywhere."

"Okay, thanks." And with that, he crept out of my office.

"Very intimidating." Winky nodded his approval. "Psycho killer comes naturally to you, doesn't it?"

***

I'd read and re-read Helen Drewmore's journal, but I was still unsure what it all meant. I deliberately hadn't told anyone else about the real reason for my trips to CASS, but now it was time to get someone else's take on the contents of the journal. Maybe a fresh pair of eyes would see something that I'd missed. And what could be better than one fresh pair of eyes, than two pairs?

I took a deep breath, and called Aunt Lucy.

"Hi, Jill. You only just caught me. I've been out with Barry."

"I wanted to talk to you and Grandma together if that's possible?"

"Is something wrong?"

"No—err—no. I just need some advice."

"What about?"

"It's kind of complicated. It would be better if I told you when I get there. Is Grandma around, do you know?"

"She was earlier. She gave me a lecture about pruning my roses. Would you like me to nip next door to check?"

"If you don't mind. If she's in and has time to spare, will you let me know, and I'll pop straight over?"

"Will do. I'll ring you back in a couple of minutes."

While I was waiting for a call back, I heard Dexter leaving. I'd been very hard on him, which was a little unfair considering his relationship with Jules was no different to mine and Jack's.

My phone rang; it was Aunt Lucy, confirming that Grandma was there with her.

"I'm on my way." I grabbed the journal, and magicked myself over to Aunt Lucy's house.

"This had better be good," Grandma said. "I was planning to lance the boil on my big toe."

"I'm sorry to be a bother."

"Take no notice of her, Jill." Aunt Lucy shot Grandma a look. "We're here for you whenever you need us."

"What's the book?" Grandma gestured to the journal.

"I haven't been completely honest with either of you about my recent trips to CASS."

"I knew it," Grandma said. "I knew you were up to something."

"Let her tell the story, Mother."

"I've been trying to find out who this man and woman are." I opened the locket. "I couldn't shake the feeling that I'm somehow connected to them. The first time I went to CASS, I sensed that I knew the place, even though I'd never been there before."

"It's called déjà vu." Grandma shrugged. "I get it all the time."

"It was more than that. When the pouchfeeder snatched the young boy, I was able to head it off by using a hidden passageway that no one knew existed. How did I know it was there?"

"What does any of this have to do with that book?" Grandma's patience was clearly wearing thin.

"I've been back to CASS a couple of times, and while I was there, I saw the two people in my locket."

"They're at CASS?" Aunt Lucy said.

"Yes — err — no — err — what I mean to say is that they're not *actually* there."

"You're making even less sense than you usually do," Grandma grumbled. "And I wouldn't have thought that was possible."

"What I saw was just a memory. At least, I think that's what it was. The young woman is Braxmore's daughter, Juliet."

"Braxmore?" That seemed to get Grandma's attention.

"Yes. And the young man is Charles Wrongacre's son, Damon. They'd planned to marry, but Braxmore wouldn't allow it."

"How can you possibly know all of this?" Grandma said.

"It was as though I was in the room with them. Another woman was there too: Helen Drewmore was Juliet's handmaid and companion. This is her journal."

"How did you get hold of that?" Grandma asked.

"I traced Helen's granddaughter, Cynthia. This journal is the reason I wanted to talk to both of you. I've read it a dozen times, and I'm still not sure what it means for me."

"For you?" Grandma snatched the journal. "Why should it mean anything for you?"

"You'll see when you read it."

Grandma flicked it open, and then looked up at me. "You'd better make yourself scarce while we read it."

"I thought you might need me to explain—"

"I think Lucy and I are both capable of understanding a journal without your help. Why don't you go to Cuppy C, and we'll call you when we're done?"

"I didn't actually expect you to do it right now."

"There's no time like the present; then I can get back to my boil."

"Okay. Thanks."

"What are you waiting for? Off you go."

***

Had I done the right thing in showing the journal to Aunt Lucy and Grandma? What would they make of it? These and a dozen other questions were swimming around my mind as I walked over to Cuppy C, which probably explained why I didn't spot Miles Best until it was too late to avoid him.

"Jill, I'm glad I've bumped into you."

"That makes one of us, then."

"I deserve that."

"Was there something you wanted?"

"Only to apologise once again for my behaviour, and to ask for your forgiveness."

"How stupid do you think I am, Miles?" I laughed. "We've been here before. You've already proven that your word and apologies are worthless."

"I don't blame you for feeling that way, but hopefully time will prove I've changed."

"And what has brought about this miraculous transformation?"

"I have a new girlfriend; her name is Cindy."

"Does Mindy know?"

"Yes. In fact, Cindy is a friend of Mindy's."

"I'm very pleased for you both, but now I have to be going because I have a rendezvous with a blueberry muffin."

"If you come into Best Cakes, you can have a muffin and coffee on the house, by way of an apology. You'll get to meet Cindy too."

"Thanks, but no thanks. I'll stick with Cuppy C."

The twins were wearing matching maternity dresses.

"Hello, you two. Isn't it a bit early to be wearing those?"

"Never too early." Amber was just as radiant as the last time I'd seen her. "They're so comfortable."

"What can I get for you, Jill?" Pearl asked. "Your usual?"

"Please. I'm starving. Guess who just collared me on the way over here?"

"Grandma? She didn't want you to lance her boil, did she?"

"No, thank goodness. It was Miles Best; he apologised to me again, and even offered me a free coffee and muffin."

"He's up to something."

"That's what I thought. He says he has a new girlfriend."

"Shush!" Amber put her finger to her lips. "Mindy's over there."

I followed her gaze to see Mindy, seated by the window.

"According to Miles," I whispered. "His new girlfriend, Cindy, is a friend of Mindy's."

"Poor Mindy," Amber said.

"I never thought I'd hear you say that. Incidentally, I've been meaning to ask the two of you—what will you do about Cuppy C?"

"How do you mean?" Pearl passed me the coffee and muffin.

"When the babies are born. Are you planning to keep the shop on, and come back to work, or will you sell up?"

"We haven't decided yet," Amber said. "We both like the idea of being stay-at-home mums, but Cuppy C is our baby too. We're going to have to give it a lot of thought."

"Jill!" Mindy called to me. "Do you have a minute?"

"Excuse me, you two. I'd better see what she wants."

"Sorry to trouble you, Jill," Mindy said. "I saw you talking to Miles. I just wondered if he'd said anything about me."

"Did you know that he's seeing someone else?"

"So I heard. He's supposedly dating Cindy, isn't he?"

"*Supposedly?*"

"He doesn't even like her; he never has. He's only doing it because she's one of my best friends. He thinks he can make me jealous, but he's got another think coming."

"Good for you."

"Why don't you join me for a few minutes?"

"Sure. Why not?"

We ended up chatting for over half an hour. Mindy was a much nicer person when she was away from Miles Best. I just hoped she'd have the resolve not to go back to him.

A couple of minutes after Mindy had left, Daze made an appearance.

"Would you like another drink, Jill?"

"Yes, please." I thought I might as well because I had no idea how long I might be waiting for Grandma's call.

"There you go." She handed me the latte, and joined me at the table.

I took out my purse to pay her.

"Put that away. This is on me, by way of a thank you for your help with the gargoyles."

"Did you catch them?"

"Yes. They're all banged up in Candlefield. We also managed to recover some of their haul, and return it to the rightful owners. I was so relieved to get out of that fish and chip shop. If I'd had to spend another day in there, I would have handed in my notice. Blaze too."

"I'm pleased I was able to help. Do you think I could pick your brain on something?"

"You can try."

"I just wanted your take on which sup/human relationships seem to work best?"

"I'm not sure I'm the best person to ask for relationship advice."

"I meant which ones are least likely to fall foul of the rules governing such relationships. You guys are responsible for arresting sups who reveal their true identities to their human partners. I just wondered if it's more likely to happen with a witch or wizard, or a vampire or werewolf."

"Is this about you and Jack?"

"No. Actually, what prompted the question is that my PA has started dating a werewolf."

"Mrs V?"

"No." I laughed. "The other one: Jules. I also know two humans who are dating vampires. I just wondered if certain pairings were more prone to fall foul of the rules than others?"

"The only thing I have to go on is the number of arrests we make. We take far more witches and wizards back to Candlefield than we do vampires or werewolves."

"That's not very encouraging."

"To be fair, I'd say that there are far more witches and wizards in relationships with humans than there are vampires or werewolves. The other problem is that a lot of witches and wizards just can't keep their magic in their shorts."

Just then my phone rang; it was Grandma.

"We're ready for you."

"Okay. I'm on my way." I slurped down the rest of the coffee. "Sorry, Daze, I have to run."

Chapter 22

When I arrived back at Aunt Lucy's, she was just pouring the three of us a cup of tea.

"I'd offer you a cupcake, but I imagine you had a muffin at Cuppy C?"

"Actually, they were all out of blueberry muffins."

What? A little white lie never hurt anyone.

"Have you both read the journal?" I asked, as the three of us took our seats around the dining table.

"We have." Grandma yawned. "It's never going to become a bestseller."

"What do you make of it?"

"Well, I—" Aunt Lucy began, but she didn't get any further because Grandma raised her hand.

"Before we have our say, why don't you tell us what you make of it?"

She'd put me on the spot.

"I don't know."

"You must have some thoughts on it."

"Okay." I took a few moments to compose myself. "If the journal is correct, Charles Wrongacre tried to save his daughter and Damon by developing a spell that would allow them to return again."

"Are you talking about reincarnation?" Aunt Lucy said.

"I suppose so."

"Carry on," Grandma urged.

"The first time Damon came back from the dead, he sought out Juliet, and believed he'd found her in Magna Mondale. But it was obvious to him that Magna didn't remember him or their former life together. Damon went in search of Helen Drewmore, and found her daughter,

Freda. She gave him the locket, which he gave to Magna Mondale. The following day, Damon was murdered. When Magna returned the locket, Freda offered to show her the journal, but Magna declined the offer because she was sure that Damon had got the wrong person. When Damon returned from the dead a second time, he once again retrieved the locket, and brought it to me. Not long after that, I found him dead—he'd been murdered."

"You've told us what happened." Grandma sighed. "But not what it means."

"That's because I don't know what it means."

"Rubbish." She thumped the table. "Tell us what you think."

"Okay. I think that Juliet Braxmore returned from the dead, first as Magna Mondale, and then—" I hesitated.

"Then what?"

"As me. What else am I meant to think?"

"Didn't I tell you, Lucy?" Grandma turned to her daughter. "I knew that's what she thought."

"What other explanation could there be?" I said.

"You're missing a couple of vital points." Grandma picked up the journal, and flicked through the pages. "Here! Read this section carefully."

I did as she said, but I wasn't sure what she was getting at. I shook my head.

"It says that the spell was first cast on Damon, and then on Juliet. It also says that Charles Wrongacre was concerned that the spell hadn't worked properly the second time because he was interrupted by Braxmore's men."

"I remember that, but why is that significant?"

"Because of what happened subsequently. When

Damon returned, he looked identical each time. And, not only did he look the same, but at a certain age, he began to remember his past life."

"But, I don't look anything like Juliet Braxmore, and from what I've seen, neither did Magna Mondale."

"Precisely." Grandma nodded. "And neither of you had any memory of Damon, or of a past life. Have you ever stopped to wonder why he picked out you and Magna when neither of you look like Juliet?"

"I hadn't really thought about it."

"I did. Juliet Braxmore was reportedly one of the most powerful witches of her time, so when Damon couldn't find anyone who looked like Juliet, he sought out the most powerful witches alive: the first time that was Magna Mondale; the second time it was you."

"But what does all that mean? Who am I? Am I Juliet Braxmore or Magna Mondale?"

"You're neither of them. This is really very simple: you're Jill Gooder. The spell that Charles Wrongacre cast on his daughter didn't work—at least, not as he'd intended it to. Unlike Damon, she was not reincarnated. However, it does appear that something of her—let's call it her spirit—somehow found a new home, not once but twice. The first time in Magna Mondale, and the second time in you. That would explain why both you and Magna were blessed with such extraordinary powers."

I took my first drink of tea, which by now was almost cold. "Aunt Lucy? You haven't said anything yet? What do you think?"

"I don't think any of us can ever know for sure, but I do believe that the explanation your grandmother has come up with is the one that makes the most sense. What about you? How do you feel about all this?"

"Confused mainly. I'd like to think that Grandma is right. I'm Jill Gooder. Not Magna Mondale or Juliet Braxmore."

"There is one unknown that worries me," Grandma said.

"What's that?"

"Braxmore."

"Why worry about him? He's gone."

"Has he, though? Are you sure about that? Someone killed Magna Mondale, and Damon — twice. And someone sent TDO after you. Who's to say it wasn't Braxmore?"

"How could he possibly be alive after all this time?"

"I don't think you can ignore the possibility."

"If he was, then he would have come after me again, wouldn't he?"

"He still might."

"What do you think I should do?"

"About Braxmore? There's nothing you can do except be vigilant at all times. You must never let your guard down."

"I meant about Juliet and Magna. I feel as though I owe them some kind of debt."

"Nonsense. The only person you owe anything to now is yourself. You need to start to live your own life, and forget what may or may not have happened in the past. That's gone now, and isn't something you can change."

***

When I got back to the office, Jules was still floating on cloud Dexter.

"What did you think of him, Jill?"

"Dexter? He seems nice enough."

"Don't you think he's a hunk?"

"I guess so, but physique isn't everything. Personality is just as important."

"Of course. He's really nice—very sweet. He's taking me to his favourite pub tonight—it's called The Howling. I've never been there before."

I had. It was a favourite haunt of werewolves. The last time I'd been there was when I'd managed to thwart Boris Breakskull's plans for the werewolves to take over the human world.

"If memory serves me right, it's a bit of a dive; it attracts some unsavoury characters. Just be careful."

"I'll be okay. I have Dexter to protect me."

There was no sign of Winky anywhere in my office. Big Gordy's money was due today, so maybe Winky had decided to take it to him rather than wait for him to collect it.

I was on the point of calling it a day, and heading home, when the temperature dropped.

"Jill. Are you okay? You look a little washed out." It was my father.

"I'm okay—just a little tired."

"I know just the thing to cheer you up. Come with me." He held out his hand.

"I'm done in, Dad. I'm not really in the mood for—"

"Nonsense." He took my hand. "This will do you the world of good. You'll need to magic yourself to GT with me, though. You can do that, can't you?"

"Sure. Where are we going?"

"You'll see. Come with me."

I cast the spell, and held onto his hand. When we arrived in GT, Blodwyn was waiting for us. "I'm sorry about this, Jill. I tried to tell him this was a bad idea."

Only then, did I realise we were standing right outside my mother's house.

"Dad? What are we doing here?"

"Come on." My father grabbed Blodwyn's hand, and led both of us up the driveway, and around the back of the house.

"What do you want?" My mother yelled at my father, and then she spotted me. "Jill?"

I shrugged.

"I bought three tickets earlier, from Alberto." My father produced them from his pocket. "Shall we begin the tour?"

I'm convinced that if I hadn't been there, my mother would have taken one of the gnomes and broken it over my father's head. Instead, she was forced to take us on a guided tour of the garden.

"What's this one called, Darlene?" My father pointed to a gnome with a fishing rod, next to the ornamental well.

"His name is Rod."

"Rod?" He laughed. "I have to hand it to Alberto. He has a sense of humour."

"I did try to talk him out of this," Blodwyn whispered.

"What about this one?" My father pointed again.

"That one is called Jill."

He glanced at me. "Oh, yes. Now, I see the resemblance. It's the nose, isn't it?"

If my mother didn't kill him, I probably would.

What? Yes, of course I know he's already dead.

Fifteen minutes later, and it was obvious that my mother was rushing through the tour just as fast as she could. I couldn't say that I blamed her.

"Is that one called Darlene?" My father pointed to a large gnome, wearing a pink dress.

"No, it isn't." My mother was livid. "Its name is Barbara."

"Oh? I thought it might be named after you."

"And why would you think that?"

"It's just that she has a big mouth, don't you think?"

"Right!" My mother picked up an empty plant pot from the pile next to the bench.

"Don't throw that, Darlene!" My father raised his hand, but it was too late—the plant pot was already winging its way towards him. He managed to duck just in time. "There's no need—" He wasn't quick enough to avoid the second one.

"Come on." I grabbed Blodwyn's arm. "This isn't our battle."

"What's going on out here?" Alberto appeared at the back door.

"Nice to see you, Alberto." I dragged Blodwyn past him and down the driveway.

"I can't apologise enough, Jill." Blodwyn was clearly enraged by what she'd just witnessed.

"It isn't your fault. My father is behaving like a child; he should know better. I have to get back. Will you be okay?"

"I will be, but your father won't. When your mother has finished with him, he'll have me to reckon with."

***

I magicked myself back to Washbridge, and then drove home. Normally, on a Friday night, I could look forward to a long, restful weekend, but not today. Saturday evening was the Ever ballroom dancing competition. No doubt Jack would spend all of tomorrow preparing for that. And then, on Sunday, I'd arranged to travel on the Washbridge Flyer.

Weekends just didn't get any better than that.

When I walked into the house, I could hear voices. Jack was talking to Megan.

"Hi, Megan." I tried to sound more upbeat than I felt.

"Megan came around to ask if she could borrow a tablecloth," Jack said.

"I'm sorry to ask, Jill, but I want to make a good impression on Ryan's parents, and the only tablecloth I own is a bit shabby. I'd buy a new one, but I had to have the van serviced, so I'm pretty skint at the moment."

"No problem. We only have three, but you're welcome to borrow one of those." I opened the drawer next to the sink. "There you go." I placed them on the kitchen table.

"The green one would be ideal. Is it alright for me to borrow that?"

"You mean the chartreuse one."

"Sorry?"

"Just my little joke. Help yourself."

"Thanks, Jill."

"No problem. I hope the dinner goes okay."

"Me too." She started for the door, but then hesitated. "Did you find your budgie, Jack?"

"Budgie?" He looked puzzled.

"Joey."

Jack looked at me, and I winked at him. "You found him, didn't you, Jack?"

"Err—yeah. Joey—err—yeah, I found him, thanks."

"That's great news. It's horrible when a pet goes missing."

As soon as Megan was out of the door, Jack turned to me. "Budgie?"

"It's a long story. I don't want to bore you."

"Go ahead. Bore me—I have all night."

"Right. Okay, well, Kathy rang me this morning to say that she'd lost her wedding ring. She thought it might have fallen off when she came over for the barbecue, so she asked if I'd look for it."

"Right? What does that have to do with a budgie?"

"That's a good question. Kathy said she'd spent a lot of time leaning against Megan's fence, so when I'd finished searching our back garden, I climbed over into Megan's to take a look in there. Anyway, long story short, Megan came back home while I was still in her garden."

"So, you told her you were looking for a budgie?"

"That's right."

"Called Joey?"

"Correct."

"Why not just tell her that you were looking for Kathy's wedding ring?"

"Kathy said I mustn't tell anyone in case it got back to Peter."

"Err—right, but won't she have to tell him sooner or later?"

"Not now. Crisis averted. Kathy rang this afternoon to tell me she'd found the ring."

"Where was it?"

"Where?"

"Yeah. Where did she find it?"

"In — err — the — err — jelly. She'd made some for the kids and it must have fallen into it. It's a good thing she noticed the ring before one of the kids swallowed it."

"I guess so. Right, I'm going upstairs to get changed."

"Okay."

What? Come on — the 'missing wedding ring in the jelly' story was sheer genius.

Chapter 23

"Jill! I need your help. It's urgent!" Jack called from upstairs.

It was Saturday, and he'd been on edge all day, and all because of some stupid ballroom dancing competition. I'd tried to take his mind off it by suggesting we go for a drive into the countryside for lunch, but he'd said he couldn't afford the time.

When I walked into the bedroom, I found him standing in front of the full-length mirror. He was holding a bow tie next to his shirt collar.

"What's the emergency?"

He turned to face me. "Which bow tie do you think? The blue? or green?"

"Which one do you prefer?"

"Green, I think."

"Me too. Green is definitely the one."

"But then, maybe blue is better?"

"Blue, yeah. Definitely blue."

"Are you sure? The green one does look good."

Oh boy. "Why not take both? You could swap them halfway through the evening."

"That's a brilliant idea!" He came over and planted a kiss on my cheek. "Why didn't I think of that?"

"No problem." I started towards the stairs.

"Aren't you getting ready yet?"

"We don't have to be there for two hours."

"You have to look your best. You are accompanying one of the judges, after all."

"No one is going to notice me. They'll all be too busy watching the dancers. You haven't forgotten that you have to let Mrs V and Armi win, have you?"

"I'm not going to — "

"Kidding. Just kidding."

I wasn't really. If I thought I could get away with it, I'd employ a little magic chicanery to influence the result, but with Grandma taking part in the competition, that was a non-starter.

I realised that Jack was right. As a judge's partner, I really ought to make the effort, so I spent the next hour sprucing myself up, and although I say it myself, I looked pretty darn good.

"Jill! Are you ready?" he called from downstairs. "We have to get going."

"Ta-da!" I stood at the top of the stairs, and did a little twirl.

"Have you seen my keys?"

"Never mind your keys. What about me?" I did a second twirl.

"You look nice. Oh, I remember. I put them on the kitchen table."

Nice? Was that all I got? I might as well have thrown on jeans and a jumper.

"Found them." He waved the keys. "Come on. We're going to be late."

"How will we be late? There's an hour until it starts."

"There might be a queue at the toll bridge, or a million other things that could delay us."

"Like a zombie apocalypse or a werewolf invasion?"

"Now you're just being silly."

During the journey into Washbridge, I had to endure more big band music, as Jack 'got into the mood'. Once we'd parked, he practically dragged me across town to Ever.

"Slow down! I can't run in these heels."

"If we're late your grandmother will kill me."

Interest in the competition was so great that, when we arrived, there was already a queue outside, even though there was over half an hour until the doors officially opened.

Jack caught Grandma's eye, and she came to unlock the door for us.

"About time!" She tapped her watch.

"Sorry." Jack apologised.

"Go through to my office. Your fellow judges are in there."

Jack set off, and I was about to follow when Grandma grabbed my arm.

"Where do you think you're going?"

"I was just—"

"You said you'd help tonight."

"Yes, I know, and I will. Just tell me what you want me to do."

"The first thing you need to do is get changed."

"Why? What's wrong with this outfit? I spent ages getting ready."

"That's as maybe, but the punters need to know who is on the staff. I've got a uniform for you to wear."

"What kind of uniform?"

"Go through to the staff room. It's in there."

"But, Grandma—"

It was too late; she was headed towards the judges' soiree. That woman had a nerve, expecting me to wear some stupid waitress' outfit, but it was too late to back out now.

When I stepped into the staff room, I was greeted by Kathy, Maria and three other Everettes.

"Hi, Jill. We've been waiting for you." Kathy had a stupid grin on her face.

"Kathy? I didn't realise you'd be working tonight."

"Your grandmother roped us all in."

"She said I'd find my uniform in here."

"Here it is." Kathy held up the red trouser suit. "You're an honorary Everette for the evening."

"Is this a wind-up?"

It wasn't.

As if it wasn't bad enough that I looked like an over-ripe tomato in front of the Broom TV cameras, my trousers were an inch too short.

"Hey! What are you doing?" I tried to grab the phone from Kathy.

"Just taking a photo of you."

"Don't you dare. I've never made fun of you for having to wear that horrible uniform."

"Not much. Revenge is sooo sweet."

Just then, Grandma opened the outer doors, and the crowd filed in. For the next thirty minutes, my feet never touched the ground, as I hurried back and forth between the bar and the tables. Meanwhile, Jack was seated at the top table, laughing and joking with his fellow judges, one of whom I recognised. It was Maurice Montage, dance instructor, and sometime interior designer.

During a lull in proceedings, I managed to fight my way over to where Jack was seated.

"Jill? What are you wearing?" He grinned.

"It isn't funny."

"Hello there." Maurice leaned forward. "I almost didn't recognise you. Have you given up the P.I. business?"

"No, I haven't. I'm just helping out tonight."

"In that case, could you get me a Babycham? What about you, Jack?"

"Just a soda water, please, my little lady-in-red." He laughed.

I came this close to smacking him around the head with my tray.

As Grandma was taking part in the competition, she'd brought in an MC to oversee proceedings. The old wizard, who introduced himself as Brad Noakes, called the room to order by tapping loudly on the microphone.

"Ladies and gentlemen. Welcome to the Ever Ballroom inaugural competition. Mirabel Millbright, the esteemed owner of this fine establishment, has done me the great honour of asking me to act as your MC tonight. My first duty is to introduce your judges: On the right is Mr Maurice Montage. Maurice is a veteran of the ballroom dancing scene; he has won numerous national medals. In the centre, is Eliza Slowstep, another national competition winner, whom many of you will recognise from TV's Dancing To Win. And finally, we have our local judge, Jack Maxwell. Jack was until recently a member of the Washbridge police force, but now works out of West Chipping. He has won numerous regional dancing awards, and is known particularly for his paso doble. Please give it up for your judges."

The crowd clapped enthusiastically.

"And finally," the MC continued. "Refreshments are

available at the table from the Everettes—you can't miss them—they're the ones in the delightful red trouser suits. And so, without further ado, let the competition commence."

The next couple of hours were something of a blur. The other Everettes and I were run off our feet, so none of us had much of a chance to watch the dancing. Fortunately, by the time it reached the penultimate round, things had quietened down a little. By then, most people had had enough to drink, so I was able to watch the final stages of the competition.

Grandma's partner was an old guy by the name of Laurence Roper. There was no doubt the two of them could dance, but they were also taking no prisoners, knocking other competitors out of the way to ensure they were always in the judges' line of sight. It was a ruthless but effective tactic that had seen them through to the final. Joining them there were Mrs V and Armi who had won their place without any of the underhand moves employed by Grandma.

If there was any justice in the world, Mrs V and Armi would take the trophy. Now that there were only two couples left on the dance floor, Grandma and her partner would no longer be able to use their bullyboy tactics because they would be seen and disqualified by the judges.

"Who's your money on?" Kathy joined me on the edge of the dance floor, just as the final was about to commence.

"It had better be Mrs V and Armi. Have you seen how Grandma and her partner have been knocking the other couples out of the way?"

"Yes, I saw them. It's a pity the judges didn't. Surely, Jack will give it to Mrs V and Armi, won't he?"

"Only if he thinks they deserve it. Jack is incorruptible—more's the pity. I tried to get him to promise he'd make sure that Mrs V would win, but he wasn't having any of it. He's such a paragon of virtue. I don't know where he gets it from."

"Not from you; that's for sure."

"Ladies and gentlemen!" The MC took to the mic again. "We now come to the grand final between Mirabel Millbright and her partner, Laurence Roper, and Annabel Versailles and her partner, Joseph Armitage."

"Go Mrs V!" I yelled.

Grandma glared at me.

"You're in for it now," Kathy whispered.

"I don't care. Go Armi!"

The audience was so engrossed in the final that Kathy and I were able to watch it uninterrupted.

"I think Mrs V and Armi just edged it," Kathy said when the music stopped.

"They were the best by far. They're bound to win."

The three judges scribbled their decision onto slips of paper, and then passed them to the MC.

"Ladies and gentlemen, we have a winner. With three votes to none, I am pleased to announce that the winners of the inaugural Ever ballroom dancing competition are Mirabel Millbright and Laurence Roper."

The crowd seemed stunned momentarily, but then broke into polite applause. Grandma and her partner stepped forward to receive their trophy from Eliza Slowstep.

"Get in there!" Grandma shouted, as she and Laurence held the trophy aloft.

Once the competition had ended, the crowd soon slipped away. I was back in the staff room with Kathy and the other Everettes.

"I never want to see this horrible thing again!" I threw the trouser suit onto the floor.

"It's okay for you," Kathy said. "I have to wear this stupid thing every day."

"I'll never make fun of you again."

"Yes, you will."

"You're right. I will."

"I still don't know how your grandmother managed to win. You need to have a serious word with Jack."

"Don't worry. I intend to."

"You should have kept the trouser suit on," Jack said when he and I were in the car. "I thought you looked sexy in it."

"I'm not talking to you."

"I'm sorry I made fun of the Everette outfit."

"Not because of that. How could you vote for Grandma to win the final?"

"I didn't."

"It was three votes to nil. You must have."

"I suppose I must have, but I intended to vote for Mrs V. I distinctly remember putting the tick against her name, but—err—well, I must have made a mistake. The funny thing is that when I was speaking to Maurice afterwards, he said exactly the same thing. He was convinced he'd voted for Mrs V and Armi. Strange, eh?"

"Why didn't you say anything to the head judge?"

"I did, but she said that it wasn't possible to change the vote. She even showed me my voting slip, and I had put the tick next to your grandmother's name. What could I do?"

That cheating, underhanded, despicable woman! She must have somehow used magic to change the voting slips. Were there no depths to which she would not sink?

Chapter 24

It was Sunday morning, and I was gobbling down cornflakes.

"Do you have to work today?" Jack was at the breakfast bar—still in his PJs. "I thought it would be nice to get lunch out."

"*Now* you want to get lunch? I tried to get you to go for lunch yesterday."

"I was too busy preparing for the dancing competition."

"You mean the competition where you denied Mrs V her rightful trophy?"

"Don't make me feel any worse than I already do."

"Why not? Can you imagine the stick I'll get from her tomorrow? And justifiably so."

"Come on. It's a beautiful day. We could go up to the Angler's Rest. You know you love their Sunday lunch."

"I'd like nothing better, but I'm working. I need to take a trip on the Washbridge Flyer to see if it provides me with any clues on the murders."

"I'm surprised it's running while the murderer is still at large."

"I don't think they can afford to close it down. From what I can gather, their finances are already stretched to the limit."

"I suppose I could always give Kathy and Peter a call to see if they fancy going for lunch."

"Why not? I wouldn't want you to feel bad about me, working my fingers to the bone while you three stuff yourselves."

"We won't."

Sheesh!

***

There was a huge crowd outside the station, so it took me a few minutes to spot Desmond Sidings.

"Jill, I was beginning to think you weren't going to make it."

"Sorry I'm late. I forgot to set the alarm clock. Is it always this busy?"

"I wish. Most of these people don't have tickets—they just turned up on spec. We could have sold out four times over. I suppose it's all the publicity we've been attracting. Come on. We'd better climb on board or we'll be left behind."

He led the way onto the platform, and into the front carriage, which although full, was surprisingly tranquil.

"I thought you said the press were on the train?"

"They are, but they're all in the rear carriage with that nuisance, West."

"Thomas West? I thought he'd quit?"

"He did. He's booked a ticket as a passenger, and invited all his press buddies along. I thought about turning him away, but that would have given the press an even bigger story."

"Jill!" A familiar voice called. It was Stanley Sidcup. "This is yours." He patted the seat next to him.

"I'll leave you to it, Jill." Desmond started down the aisle towards the buffet car. "Give me a shout if you need anything."

"Recent events haven't put you off, then, Stanley?"

"It will take more than a few murders to scare me

away." He laughed. "But I am hoping for an uneventful trip today. Have you made any progress with your investigation?"

"Not really. That's why I'm here. I thought it might give me some inspiration."

The train jolted, and we were on our way. Steam plumed past the window as we headed out into the countryside.

"Have you travelled on a steam train before, Jill?"

"I don't think so."

"You'll love it. Before you know it, you'll be signing up for a season ticket."

"I seriously doubt that. I do have a neighbour who is into trains in a big way. I'm sure he'd love this."

Stanley and I chatted about nothing in particular for the next ten minutes, then I went through to the buffet car. I wanted to grab a word with Stephen Pearce, the replacement guard who had taken over after Thomas West had resigned.

There were several people waiting at the counter, and I didn't think the other customers would appreciate my pushing in, so I joined the back of the queue.

"What can I get for you?" The young man looked and sounded harassed.

"Just a cup of tea, please."

"Milk and sugar?"

"Yes, please. I take it this is your second trip on The Flyer?"

"Err—yes?"

"Sorry, I should have introduced myself. I'm Jill Gooder. I'm a P.I."

"Oh, right. Mr Sidings mentioned you'd be on board

today."

"I assume you're hoping this trip is less eventful than the last time?"

"You could say that." He managed a smile.

"Did you see anything unusual on your first outing?"

"Nothing at all. I'd been thrown in at the deep-end, and had virtually no training, so it took me all of my time to keep pace with the orders. I didn't even know where the additional stores were kept. The first I knew that anything had happened was when we arrived back at the station, and I heard that someone had been murdered."

He handed me my tea. There was no possibility of quizzing him further because a queue had built up behind me.

"Okay. Thanks, Stephen."

The noise level in the rear carriage was much higher, and it was all centred around one particular table where Thomas West was the focus of attention. A camera crew and numerous members of the press: photographers and reporters, were crowded around him. I walked over until I was close enough to hear what was being said.

"You must be nervous to be back aboard The Flyer, Thomas?" a male reporter with way too much ear hair shouted. "Aren't you scared that it might happen again?"

"Terrified." Thomas grinned; he certainly didn't appear to be frightened.

"Is that why you quit, Mr West?" a female reporter asked. "Were you afraid you might become the next victim?"

"Partly that, but mainly I wanted to return to my first passion. You may not know this, but I'm actually an author. I had a book published many years ago. I've decided to return to writing, and I already have my new book outlined."

"What's it about, Thomas?"

"It's a murder mystery. A sort of whodunit, I suppose. The story was inspired by recent events."

"Do you have a publisher lined up?"

"Nothing has been signed yet, but there's been a lot of interest."

I'd heard enough of this publicity-seeking braggart, so I pushed past the press huddle, and made my way to the back of the carriage where I'd spotted a familiar face.

Barbara Hawthorne was seated at a table right next to the guard's van.

"Thorny?"

"Hello there. Are you still investigating the murders?"

"Yes. I thought a trip aboard The Flyer might help."

"I'm beginning to regret coming today. That horrible little man has already spoiled two trips for me, and now he seems intent on spoiling another. I can hardly hear myself think with that crowd of hyenas hovering around him."

"I just overheard him say that he was writing a new book based on The Flyer murders."

"How tacky. Unfortunately, it's just the type of trash that publishers will lap up these days."

"Mrs Hawthorne." Stephen Pearce appeared behind me. "You left your bag in the buffet car." He passed it to her.

"Thank you very much, young man."

"No problem. I'd better get back to work."

She turned to me. "I'd forget my head if it were loose."

I tried the door to the guard's van, but it was locked. "Do you always sit in this same seat?"

"I do. Every trip."

"Did you see anyone go in or out of the guard's van on the trip when Carol Strand was murdered?"

"Yes, the guard." She pointed. "He knocked the wine out of my hand when he hurried past me."

I looked up, expecting to see Stephen Pearce on his way back to the buffet car, but he'd already left the carriage. It wasn't Pearce she'd been pointing to; it was Thomas West.

Bingo!

We were just about to pull into the station when a blood-curdling scream came from the far end of the carriage. I was the first to react; I rushed up the aisle, and past the press pack who were now starting to register what they'd heard.

"It must be another murder!" someone yelled.

"Quick! Check the toilet!"

I hurried through to the small section of corridor where the toilet was located, but I wasn't the first one on the scene. Desmond Sidings was already standing outside the toilet door.

"Are you alright in there?" He hammered on the door.

The press had followed me, and were trying to push past.

"Stay back!" I barked at them.

"Hello?" Desmond banged on the door again.

"There's no loo paper in here." A meek voice came back. "Could you pass me some, please?"

Once we were back in the station, I skipped off the train,

and hurried back to the car. The journey on The Flyer had proven to be worthwhile after all, even if it had meant sacrificing lunch. At long last, I had something to go on. Hopefully, tomorrow, I'd be able to put my hunch to the test.

***

When I got back to the house, Peter's car was parked on the road.

"Look who's back!" Jack said, as I joined the three of them in the lounge.

"I wasn't expecting to find the whole gang here."

"We had a late lunch at the Angler's." Kathy had a glass of wine in her hand. "It was delicious."

"I had a cheese and pickle sandwich. Thanks for asking."

"Pete's Mum has the kids, so we thought we'd come back here to make an evening of it."

"And drink my wine."

"There's plenty left, grumpy. Go and get yourself a glass."

Kathy followed me into the kitchen, and pushed the door shut behind her.

"You didn't tell me." She was grinning like a demented Cheshire cat.

"Tell you what?"

"Wedding bells."

"I'm not in the mood for your cryptic clues."

"Why didn't you tell me that you and Jack were getting married?"

"Because we're not."

"Come on, Jill. The secret's out."

"I've told you—we're not getting married. Why would you think we are?"

"Because Jack has been dropping subtle hints all afternoon."

"What kind of subtle hints?"

"Twice he came up to me, and whispered, 'wedding ring', and then winked."

"Are you sure that's what he said?"

"Yeah. He also said something else that I didn't understand. He said: Jelly."

"It must be the pills."

"What pills?"

"Jack has been suffering with really bad hay fever. The doctor gave him some stronger pills. Did he have a drink in the pub?"

"Just a small glass of beer."

"That would do it. The poor man wouldn't know what he was saying. He didn't mention pink elephants too, did he?"

"No. Why?"

"That's when you know it's really bad. When he starts talking about pink elephants."

"Oh, sorry, I had no idea."

"That's okay. Would you ask Jack if he'll come through to the kitchen?"

"Sure."

"You didn't mind me asking Kathy and Peter to come back here, did you?" Jack said.

"Of course not, but why did you mention the wedding ring thing to Kathy?"

"I was only teasing her. Peter didn't hear."

"You mustn't do it again. She's terrified that Peter will find out about it."

"Okay. My lips are sealed."

"They'd better not be." I pulled him towards me, and gave him a kiss.

***

After Kathy and Peter had left, I slipped upstairs to make a phone call.

"Is that Thomas West?" I said, in my best American accent.

"Speaking?"

"My name is Lucinda Shell. I'm with the UK office of Channel TN6. We've seen the article on the train murders, and heard about your proposed book. We thought that would make an ideal feature for our viewers back in the States."

"Really?"

"Definitely. I wondered if I might arrange an on-camera interview with you aboard the steam train. What's it called?"

"The Washbridge Flyer, but I doubt the owners would allow us to film there. I think they're rather fed up of me."

"Don't worry about that. I'm sure I'll be able to get them to agree. The problem is that we need to do this quickly if we're going to include it in this week's program."

"When did you have in mind?"

"Tomorrow morning if you can manage that?"

"Okay. What time?"

"I'll text you with the details once I've cleared it with

the train owner."

"Okay, great. See you tomorrow, then."

You most certainly will.

Chapter 25

It was Monday morning; Jack and I were in the kitchen.

"I don't like this. Not one bit," he said. "It sounds like you're putting yourself in danger unnecessarily."

"There's nothing to worry about. I'll be perfectly safe."

"Why don't you just call Susan Shay, and tell her of your suspicions?"

"Because that woman couldn't solve a murder if it was committed right in front of her."

"I think you're being a little unfair."

"Will you do what I asked or not?"

"Do I have any choice?"

"Not unless you want to be exiled to the spare bedroom."

"Tell me again what time you want me to call her."

"At ten o' clock. Tell her to get to the station at dead on ten-thirty."

"She's going to want to know why."

"I've already told you what to say. That the Washbridge Flyer murderer will be there to make a full confession."

"She'll ask who it is."

"And you'll tell her the truth: that you don't know."

"You realise this makes me look stupid, I suppose?"

"Not in Sushi's eyes, I'm sure. She's still sweet on you."

"You owe me big time for this."

"I know, and I promise you're really going to enjoy it when I pay my debt."

***

When I arrived at the office, both Jules and Mrs V were

at their desks. Mrs V looked rather crestfallen.

"Morning, everyone. Are you okay, Mrs V?"

"She's upset at losing out in the dance final," Jules answered for her.

"I'm fine," Mrs V insisted. "Just a little disappointed by the result. I really felt that Armi and I had done enough to win, but we didn't get even a single vote. I guess I must have been deluding myself."

"You did great. You were by far the better couple. Jack should have voted for you."

"That's very kind of you to say, Jill, but you're not an expert. The three judges all have lots of experience — they knew what they were doing."

"There'll be other competitions."

"I'm not so sure. Maybe it's time I hung up my dancing shoes."

Poor old Mrs V. She had so wanted to win, and she would have done if Grandma hadn't cheated.

Cheats? They make my blood boil.

What? Paintball? That wasn't the same thing at all. Ten-pin bowling? Completely different.

Anyway, moving on.

My office was still Winkyless. I'd searched high and low, but he was nowhere to be seen. The food that I'd put out for him on Friday was still in the bowl. He must have been away all weekend. Maybe he was paying his brother, Socks, a visit. He did stay over there from time to time, but it would have been nice if he'd thought to mention it to me.

***

Although we'd been on the train together the previous day, it was unlikely that West would remember or recognise me. He'd been much too caught up with entertaining the press pack to have noticed my brief appearance. But, just to be on the safe side, I'd put my hair up, and picked out a grey suit that I hadn't worn for almost five years.

What? Of course it still fit. Just about.

If this was going to work, my timing would have to be spot on.

As arranged, I met Thomas West at the station at ten o'clock. He was obviously keen because he was already there when I arrived.

"Mr West? Lucinda Shell. I'm so pleased you agreed to do this."

"My pleasure." He glanced around. "Where are the cameras?"

"The crew have got caught in traffic. They should be here in about thirty minutes. I thought you and I could run through a few things so we're ready to roll when they arrive. How does that sound?"

"Sounds good."

"Super. Why don't we get on board the train, and we can talk there?" I led the way onto the platform.

"You're sure it's okay to do the interview on the train?"

"Absolutely. I cleared it with Mr Sidings myself." I opened one of the doors in the rear carriage, and gestured that he should climb on board. "Shall we?" I pointed to the table in the centre of the carriage.

"How long will this feature be?" he asked, once we were seated.

"Thirty minutes. Well, twenty-six, to be precise. We're going to give over the whole show to this story. Our viewers love a mystery. What I'm particularly interested in is the book you're planning to publish. I believe it will be based on The Flyer murders. Does it have a title yet?"

"Nothing set in stone, but I was thinking: Death On The Flyer."

"Brilliant! I like it. Would it be possible to talk me through the plot?"

"It's only in the outline stage at the moment."

"That's okay. I'm excited to hear what you have in mind."

And off he went. He spent the next twenty-odd minutes rambling on about his book. He talked about the characters, the plot, the clever twists and turns. Somehow, I managed to look as though I gave even the smallest of monkeys.

After what seemed like an age, it was time to put the next part of my plan into action.

"I'm sorry to interrupt you, Thomas, but I wonder if we could go through to the corridor where the murders took place?"

"Err—sure—I guess so. The first two murders happened in the first carriage."

"What about the second woman who was killed? Where was her body found?"

"Near to the toilet in this carriage."

"Excellent. Let's take a look, shall we?" I stood up. "Through here?"

"Yes."

"So, this is where it happened? Is that right?"

He nodded.

I opened the toilet door, stepped inside, and closed the door behind me. "What was the name of the woman who was found in this carriage?"

"Strand. Carol Strand."

I cast the 'doppelganger' spell, and opened the door.

West took several steps backwards until he was up against the wall of the carriage.

"No! You're dead!" He was as white as a sheet, which was hardly surprising because he now found himself face-to-face with Carol Strand.

"Why did you kill me?"

"Leave me alone!"

"I hadn't done anything to you. You didn't even know me. Why did you do it?"

"I'm sorry!" His legs gave way, and he slid down to the floor.

I glanced out of the window, and much to my relief, Sushi and three police officers were walking down the platform. I waited a few moments until I heard the carriage door open, and then took another step closer to West.

"Please, leave me alone! Please!"

"Only if you tell me why you did it. Why did you kill me?"

"I'm sorry. I only did it for the book."

"You killed me for a book?"

"Yes, I'm sorry."

Just then, Sushi came through to the corridor.

"What's going on in here?"

"This gentleman wishes to confess to the murder of Carol Strand, don't you?"

Sushi looked down at the miserable figure of Thomas

West. "Is this true, Sir?"

"Yes. I'll tell you everything, but make her go away." He pointed at me.

"I think you'd better get off the train, Gooder, but don't leave the station because you and I need to talk."

I disembarked, and took a seat on a bench on the platform. Ten minutes later, West was led away in handcuffs by the uniformed officers. Sushi joined me on the bench.

"Did you get your confession?" I asked.

"He's admitted to the murder of Carol Strand, but not the first two murders. I'm not sure if he'll ever see the inside of a prison. The man is clearly deranged. He kept rambling on about seeing Carol Strand's ghost."

"Poor man."

"What I'd like to know is how come you knew he was going to confess?"

"I didn't."

"Then why did you get Jack to ask me to be here at ten-thirty?"

"Okay. I thought that once I confronted West with my suspicions that he might cave in, so I wanted you to be around if he did."

"What suspicions?"

"That this was all about a stupid book."

"What book?"

"West had a book published some years ago. From all accounts, it bombed, but he still aspired to become a best-selling author. Barbara Hawthorne, one of the season ticket holders on The Flyer, is a retired literary agent. In all innocence, she mentioned to West that the only way he'd ever attract the attention of a publisher was if he was a celebrity, or had created some kind of buzz in the media. My guess is that West was actually the first person to find Gena Shore's body."

"Are you suggesting he murdered Gena Shore, too?"

"No. I'm almost certain that Gary Shore murdered his wife because she'd just told him that she was leaving him. Gary then killed himself by jumping off the train. Instead of reporting the death, West simply picked up the knife."

"The murder weapon?"

"Yeah. He went back to the buffet car, and said nothing. Gena's body was then discovered by Don Preston."

"Why didn't West report the murder? And why did he take the knife?"

"Like I said, it was all about the book. In his warped little mind, he figured that if he could make people believe there was a serial killer stalking The Flyer, it would attract the attention of the press. And, he was right. Look at how much publicity there has been since the second murder."

"How did you know that West murdered Carol Strand?"

"He handed his notice in after the first murders. According to him, he was too traumatised to carry on in the job. On the second trip, his replacement, Stephen Pearce, was working in the buffet car."

"So?" Sushi's impatience was beginning to show.

"West still had his key to the guard's van. He must have hidden in there on the day of the second trip. He still had his uniform too. He waited until the journey was almost at an end, then he came out of the guard's van, walked up the carriage, and waited in the corridor. Carol Strand was just unlucky. Whoever had chosen to visit the toilet would have been the next victim. West killed her, dropped the knife where he knew it would be found, and then made his way back to the guard's van."

"Surely, someone would have seen him?"

"Why would they even notice. Most were too busy enjoying the trip, and even if they did happen to look up, they would have seen the uniform, but not necessarily the man."

"So how did you work out he was on board that second trip?"

"After he'd killed Carol Strand, he was in such a hurry to get back to the guard's van that he bumped into Barbara Hawthorne, causing her to spill her wine. She was the one who told me that West had been on that second trip."

Sushi took a deep breath. "That's all well and good, but I'm not sure we'll have enough to get a conviction."

"You have his confession."

"If it stands up. Once he has lawyered up, there'll be questions asked about how that confession was obtained. Once West starts spouting on about ghosts, I'm not sure what will happen. It would have been much better if you'd simply brought your suspicions to me."

"Would you have given me the time of day?"

She smiled. "Probably not."

Whether West would be convicted for the murder of Carol Strand, only time would tell. What was now certain was that Gary Shore had murdered his wife, and then taken his own life. That wasn't the result that my ex-clients, the Ganders, had been hoping for.

***

When I arrived back at my office, Mrs V looked much brighter.

"I'm pleased to see you looking happier."

"I'm fine. I don't know why I let it get to me. It was only a silly competition."

"You're not still thinking about hanging up your dancing shoes, are you?"

"No. While these old legs of mine keep going, I'll never quit dancing."

"That's the spirit." I started towards my office.

"Jill!" Jules called after me. "Before you go, will you settle a wager for us?"

"Sure. If I can."

"Mrs V reckons that you're doing an amdram production of Murder at the Vicarage, but I told her that you're doing The Unexpected Guest."

"I — err — I —"

"This youngster thinks I'm going senile," Mrs V said. "I know what you told me. It's Murder at the Vicarage, isn't it? Tell her, Jill. There's a fiver riding on this."

"I didn't say you were going senile," Jules said. "You just get things mixed up sometimes."

"Well, Jill?"

They were both staring at me — waiting for an answer.

"In fact, you're both right. It's a hybrid production called — err — The Unexpected Guest is Murdered at the Vicarage."

The two of them exchanged a puzzled look, and I took that opportunity to escape to my office where there was a cat waiting for me.

It wasn't Winky.

"Peggy? Are you okay?"

"No. I don't know where Winky is. I haven't heard from him since Friday. I thought he might be ill; that's why I came over, but then he wasn't here either. Do you know where he is?"

"I thought he might have gone to visit his brother, Socks."

"He would have told me if he had. I'm really worried, Jill."

"I'm sure he's okay. Winky knows how to look after himself."

"I'm not so sure. Will you try to find him, please?"

"Err—yes, of course. You go back home, and try not to worry too much. I'll make sure he gets in touch with you just as soon as I track him down."

"Okay, thanks." And with that, she disappeared out of the window.

I didn't like to say anything to Peggy, in case I upset her, but a horrible thought had crossed my mind. Winky was supposed to pay his gambling debt to Big Gordy on Friday. The last I'd heard, he was still a few pounds short. Winky hadn't seemed particularly worried, but what if Big Gordy had insisted on the full amount? What if it had turned nasty and Big Gordy had hurt Winky? What if Winky was lying injured somewhere?

Or worse?

I was annoyed at myself for not having thought of it sooner. If anything had happened to Winky, I'd never forgive myself.

Fortunately, I still had the phone number for his hacker friend, Tibby.

"Hello?"

"Tibby. It's Jill Gooder. I'm Winky's—"

"I know who you are. Is this urgent? I'm trying to fend off a DDOS attack."

"Sorry, but it's Winky. He's gone missing, and I think Big Gordy may have something to do with it."

"That's not good. I warned Winky about the gambling."

"Me too. Do you know where I can find Big Gordy?"

Much to my relief, he did.

The old brewery in Washbridge had been standing derelict for at least ten years. According to Tibby, Big Gordy's hideout was located in the basement of the building. The brewery was surrounded by a high fence, and patrolled by guard dogs, which made it all the more surprising that Big Gordy would choose to base himself there. I levitated over the fence, and then made myself invisible in order to bypass the dogs.

I found the steps to the basement at the rear of the building. The door at the bottom was locked, but I could hear voices coming from inside. I knocked, and moments later, a bruiser of a cat answered the door.

"What do you want?"

"I'd like to see Big Gordy."

"Is he expecting you?"

"No."

"Do one, then!"

Before he could close the door in my face, I used the 'power' spell to push it open. The force sent the cat spiralling backwards.

I was in a short corridor; the voices I'd heard seemed to be coming from behind the door at the far end.

"You can't go in there!" The cat was back on his feet, and in hot pursuit.

"Watch me."

The door was unlocked, so I stepped inside the smoke-filled room, and slammed the door closed behind me.

Sitting around the table were six cats: Big Gordy, Winky and four others. They were all holding cards, and in the centre of the table was a small pile of cash. In front of Winky was a much larger pile.

"Sorry, Big Gordy." The door-cat had followed me into the room. "She just burst in."

"Get out! I'll deal with you later," Big Gordy shouted, and then turned his attention to me. "If it isn't the pretty, young witch. Would you like us to deal you in?"

"No, thanks. I've come to get Winky."

"What are you?" Big Gordy laughed. "His nanny?"

"I'm okay here," Winky said, rather unconvincingly.

"There's an emergency. Your brother has been taken ill. You have to come straightaway."

"Oh? Right." He turned to Big Gordy. "Sorry, I have to go."

Big Gordy didn't look amused, but said nothing.

"I'll help you with that." I scooped up some of the cash that was on the table in front of Winky. He pocketed the rest.

"What's wrong with Socks?" Winky asked, as soon as we were outside.

"Nothing. I just said that to get you out of there. I know you wanted to stay, but that guy is really bad news."

"Stay?" Winky laughed. "I didn't want to stay. I've been trying to get out of there for two days, but Big Gordy doesn't like anyone to leave while they're winning. He would have kept me there until he'd won every penny back. And some more."

Rather than have to run the gauntlet of the guard dogs, I magicked us both back to my office.

"How do you cope with all that magic travel stuff?" Winky shook his head. "It makes me dizzy."

"You get used to it."

"How did you know where to find me?"

"Peggy came looking for you; she was really worried. I remembered you were due to see Big Gordy last Friday, so I figured there was a good chance you might be at his place. It was Tibby who told me where Gordy hangs out."

"Did you tell Peggy that's where you thought I was?"

"No. I didn't want to worry her."

"Good. She'd kill me if she knew where I'd been. Anyway, you can give me the rest of the cash now."

"What cash?"

ALSO BY ADELE ABBOTT

The Witch P.I. Mysteries
(A Candlefield/Washbridge Series)

Witch Is When... (Books #1 to #12)
Witch Is When It All Began
Witch Is When Life Got Complicated
Witch Is When Everything Went Crazy
Witch Is When Things Fell Apart
Witch Is When The Bubble Burst
Witch Is When The Penny Dropped
Witch Is When The Floodgates Opened
Witch Is When The Hammer Fell
Witch Is When My Heart Broke
Witch Is When I Said Goodbye
Witch Is When Stuff Got Serious
Witch Is When All Was Revealed

Witch Is Why... (Books #13 to #24)
Witch Is Why Time Stood Still
Witch is Why The Laughter Stopped
Witch is Why Another Door Opened
Witch is Why Two Became One
Witch is Why The Moon Disappeared
Witch is Why The Wolf Howled
Witch is Why The Music Stopped
Witch is Why A Pin Dropped
Witch is Why The Owl Returned
Witch is Why The Search Began
Witch is Why Promises Were Broken
Witch is Why It Was Over

Witch Is How... (Books #25 to #36)
Witch is How Things Had Changed
Witch is How Poison Tasted Good
Witch is How The Mirror Lied
Witch is How The Tables Turned
Witch is How The Drought Ended
Witch is How The Dice Fell
Witch is How The Biscuits Disappeared
Witch is How Dreams Became Reality
Witch is How Bells Were Saved
Witch is How To Fool Cats
Witch is How To Lose Big
Witch is How Life Changed Forever

Susan Hall Investigates
(A Candlefield/Washbridge Series)

Whoops! Our New Flatmate Is A Human.
Whoops! All The Money Went Missing.
Whoops! Someone Is On Our Case.

AUTHOR'S WEB SITE
http:www.AdeleAbbott.com

FACEBOOK
http://www.facebook.com/AdeleAbbottAuthor

MAILING LIST
(new release notifications only)

http:/AdeleAbbott.com/adele/new-releases/

Made in the USA
Monee, IL
31 August 2019